KATE'S HOUSE

Also by Mary Francis Shura:

Kate's Book

KATE'S HOUSE

Mary Francis Shura

AN
APPLE
PAPERBACK

SCHOLASTIC INC.
New York Toronto London Auckland Sydney

ISBN 0-590-42380-0

12 11 10 9 8 7 6 5 4 3   2 3 4 5/9

Printed in the U.S.A.   40
First Scholastic printing, March 1990

*For Martha, with my love as always,
and gratitude ten thousandfold.*

Contents

1
The Cat

Kate Alexander's father set his empty coffee cup on the makeshift table beside the covered wagon. He rose, smiled at Kate's mother, and pulled his axe from the side of the tree.

The trunk of the tree was bigger around than a man could clasp with his arms. Its upper branches disappeared into a faint smoky haze glowing with sunlight. Kate knew the sun would soon melt the mist away and turn the heavy dew under her feet into glistening jewels. Best of all, rainbows would come with the sunshine.

Back in Ohio, a rainbow was a *big* event. Kate's father would call her from the house to see that great curved band of color arching in the sky. In the Willamette Valley of Oregon, rainbows were as common as the gray squirrels that leaped about in the trees or the jays that screamed from dawn to dusk.

But as much as Kate loved the rainbows, she would have given them up to have dry feet.

Oregon was just plain too wet, that's what it was.

Back in Ohio, her father had called this "the land of milk and honey." To Kate it was more the land of rain and fog and wet stockings all the time. Even Buddy, the huge Irish wolfhound who had come all the way from Ohio with them, shook himself vigorously as he rose to stand at her father's side.

Simon and Sam Thompson, the twins who had worked with Daniel Alexander most of the way across the country, rose, too. Sam, who was the serious one, simply pulled his axe from the tree and put his hat on. Simon grinned over at Kate and twisted his face into a humorous wink.

Kate giggled softly. Her father glanced at her before turning to his wife. "Come noon you might send Kate along with something for us to eat. No point in wasting our strength coming back for it."

Kate stared at his back as he swung off through the trees. He couldn't possibly mean that! They had only been in the Willamette Valley of Oregon a few days. How could he expect her to find her way around in this endless forest of giant trees? How could *anyone* keep from getting lost in such deep, dark woods?

"I'll never find them out there," she wailed to her mother. "I'll only get lost myself."

"They'll leave a trail for you," Jane Alexander said. "But for now, you can start bringing me wash water from the river." As she spoke, she set a pot of water over the fire and began shaving flakes of lye soap into it. "You know where the buckets are."

Kate sighed and swallowed the last of her breakfast bread. She *should* know where those silly buckets hung. She had been toting water in them all the way across America. For the whole eight months they had traveled, it had been the same. Every time the wagon train stopped where there was water thin enough to pour, her mother washed clothes. Why had she thought it would be different now that they had finally reached Oregon?

But she *had* thought it would be different. She had even woken up that very morning planning to spend the day with Tildy Thompson, her best friend in the whole wide world. Tildy's mother, whose name was Belle, had "gone away" before Kate had even met Tildy. Tildy had no one to boss her around and make her work all day. The Thompsons had settled on the next claim over. They even had the roof raised on their cabin, but then, Mr. Thompson had four other sons to help him.

It was mean and ugly to be jealous of a friend, but Kate couldn't help it. It didn't seem fair for Tildy to have six brothers when she, Kate, had only one and never got to see him because he hadn't come west with them. But Tildy's brothers *did* make things more fun. Although they were all tall, dark-haired men with shining eyes and lean bodies, they were as different from each other as sugar from salt.

Buck was the oldest at twenty, a full man, bigger

and stronger than even Kate's papa. He rode a horse as if he had grown to it, and he faced up to the truth without flinching. After the twins came Jackson who was a wonder with wood. Kate tried not to remember how many coffins Jackson had carpentered for emigrants who had died along the trail. Titus was the youngest and a little bit of a tease like his brother Simon. Although he was only fifteen, Tildy said he had been a "wizard with horses" all his life.

Tildy, who loved them all in spite of pretending not to, felt that Carl was special. He didn't talk very much but whistled or sang along with whatever else he was doing. More than one night on the trail tears had sprung to Kate's eyes from the music Carl made with his fiddle.

Kate's little sister Molly had plumped herself down on a flat rock her father had brought from the river. With her doll Annabelle beside her, she was setting out her collection of stones in a circle. And talking to them.

Kate swung a bucket in each hand and looked at her mother. "Why don't the men start taking the trees down right here so we can get a house built?"

"Cabin," her mother corrected her. "I don't want you to go thinking glass windows and painted porches. This will be a cabin with just one room for a while, and rough logs on the outside."

"But they still have to take out the trees," Kate said.

4

"Only after your father has blazed his claim," her mother reminded her. "Now, are you going to bring me some water or not?"

Kate tightened her lips and started off toward the riverbank. That Molly didn't know how lucky she was to be only four years old! What a shock she was going to have when *she* turned eleven and her parents started to treat her as if she were hired help!

Kate's boots shone with moisture by the time she walked the short path to the riverbank. She set one bucket on a flat rock. Her mother and father treated her *worse* than hired help, she decided. *Hired help got paid!*

Kate squatted for a moment, watching the stream. It babbled like Molly as it coursed over its stones. Bright fish glistened in its pools. Now and then a leaf floated by, spinning like a tiny boat out of control. Something in the woods behind her smelled of spice, a sharp, clean fragrance that filled Kate's head and made her draw deep breaths.

Above and behind her, birds chirped and fluttered among the branches of the trees. Back in Ohio she had only thought of birds as singing. But living in a tent all these months and spending the last days in a forest had changed her mind. Birds talked to each other just the way people did, only without words.

In the morning like this, they seemed to be celebrating. Their songs were brighter and sweeter and wonderfully genial except when a couple of them got into an argument (just the way people did). By nightfall they were tired and cross. It almost made her giggle when they fretted and fussed at each other at twilight, very much the way she and Molly fretted at each other when they crawled into their tent at night to sleep.

Kate was filling the second bucket with water when the blue jays in the trees behind her began to scream. She looked around nervously. She knew what *that* cry was. When the blue jays screamed alarm, an enemy was near.

She stared a long time into the shaded green, trying to see what was making the noisy jays bounce from limb to limb like that. Their frantic action now and then broke off a twig or a pinecone with a cluster of needles. These clattered to the ground, adding further confusion to the clamoring of the birds and the steady voice of the river.

Once, out on the prairie, Tildy Thompson had appeared suddenly and silently, scaring Kate half out of her head. It hadn't helped that Tildy had warned her that Indian braves could sneak up silently like that. Kate's eyes hurt from staring into the green. Maybe Tildy was in there hiding, waiting to jump out at her.

"Tildy," she called in a quiet, level voice. "You there, Tildy Thompson?"

When no answer came, Kate rose swiftly, suddenly filled with panic. Tildy might *start* to sneak up on her but she wouldn't go the whole way if Kate called. She was too good a friend to do that.

Kate seized the handles of the buckets and started running back toward the camp. The water sloshed icy against the sides of her skirt. Her swift movement gave the blue jays a fresh cause for squalling. Their sharp cries pierced the air.

"Oh, shut up!" she yelled at them. "Shut that racket up this minute!"

They didn't obey, of course, but as she glanced up at them, something stirred along the dark branch of a nearby tree. It was paler than the bark of the tree and softer-looking. She caught her breath, but strangely enough, not in fear.

A great toast-colored cat lay along the branch, staring at her with eyes that looked golden in that light. His face was shaped like that of their barn cat back home in Ohio.

Tildy was a great one for telling tall tales. Sometimes it was hard for Kate to tell whether Tildy was telling the truth or some rip-roaring big fib that she had made up just for the fun of it. But she had told Kate a story about a snake that stared you in the eyes until you were hypnotized and couldn't move. Even though the cat looked directly into Kate's eyes, she didn't see danger in his look. Instead, the cat only looked curious. As she watched, he stretched a little on the branch, yawned, and put his head down as if to sleep.

She had set down her buckets without realizing it. She watched him sleep a moment, then picked them up and started off again. She had taken only a few steps when she saw Tildy standing in the path, silently watching her.

"I didn't answer when you called because I saw that cougar," Tildy said softly in that deep gravelly voice Kate had learned to like. "They eat people, you know. But they don't eat them right off. First they roll them around and play with them like a cat does with a mouse."

When Kate stared at her, trying to decide how much of this was the truth, Tildy nodded and kept going. "They kill cattle, too, and eat them. I don't mean little calves, I mean *big* animals, like oxen, even. I figured if he was going to give a big pounce off that limb and catch him a little girl for breakfast, I'd let you have that honor instead of me."

Kate laughed softly. Tildy was eleven like Kate herself, but she was shorter than Kate and sturdier. When they first met, back on the trail, Kate hadn't much liked Tildy's looks. Her face was as round as a flapjack with a pale line of freckles dusted across her cheeks and her snub of a nose.

"His eyes are yellow like yours," Kate said.

Tildy stared. "I guess I'm supposed to like being told that. Eyes like a cougar, indeed!" Her tone sounded insulted, but Kate knew she was kidding from the broad, warm smile that showed the gap between her teeth.

Tildy reached for one of the buckets, but Kate shook her head. "I have them balanced," she said. "And anyway, why should we both have wet skirts?"

Tildy looked down at her dress. "Mine could use a little water if there was soap in it. Your mother said you were helping her do the washing."

Kate made a face and nodded.

Tildy skipped to catch up. "How about I pitch in so you'll get through to play quicker?"

Kate nodded at her, grinning. "You have *good* ideas!"

2
The Woods Watcher

The sun was high above the trees when the washing was finally done and draped over bushes and tree limbs to dry.

"Now can we play?" Kate asked. Her mother, feeding fresh wood to the fire under her skillet, looked over at her. Kate sometimes wished she looked like her mother and Molly instead of having her father's red, curly hair. Molly and her mother both had the "Morrison" coloring: shining black hair, eyes as dark as night shadows, and pale white skin. The heat of the fire had turned her mother's cheeks as pretty a pink as the sprigs of roses on her bonnet.

She looked beautiful, but her expression was concerned. "Just don't go far. You'll need to carry lunch to the menfolk soon."

Tildy glanced around. "Where's that great dog of yours?"

"Buddy went off with Papa and the twins," Kate told her.

"I'd rather he was walking with us," Tildy said.

Kate laughed. "*Now* who's a scaredy-cat?" she asked. All the way from Missouri Tildy had teased her about being afraid of things. Kate knew that Tildy got scared, too; she just felt she had to act as brave as her brothers were.

Tildy flushed. "It's different here. We never saw any wildcats when we were traveling."

Kate's mother stiffened as she looked up. "What wildcats?" she asked. "What are you girls talking about?"

Through the whole trip Kate's mother had worried. She had worried about people getting sick, about their being hurt in accidents, even about wild animals eating them, or their being bitten by snakes. Kate surely didn't want her mother to get nervous and fretful like *that* again. Kate glanced at Tildy for help.

Tildy understood. She caught her lip between her teeth and her words came out lamely. "You know how people always talk about bears and wolves and wildcats."

"I know what people say," Kate's mother said. "Just don't go talking about things like that unless you've seen them."

Kate felt her face redden, hoping her mother wouldn't come right out and *ask* her if she had seen a wildcat. She couldn't possibly lie, but neither could she explain how pretty and gentle the cat had looked.

When the lunch basket was filled, Kate looked at her mother. "Now, how are we ever supposed to find those men in these woods?"

Her mother shook her head and laughed softly. "Kate Alexander! Sometimes I think you spend half your time with your ears folded shut. You've heard all this talk about our claim. We can keep our six-hundred-and-forty-acre claim only if we mark it off and till it and live here a year. You just have to follow the marks your father and the twins have been making this morning."

"That's right," Tildy said, taking one end of the basket handle. "The axe marks look bright on the dark trees. I guess that's why Paw calls these tomahawk claims. I watched him and the boys blaze our claim before you got here."

They walked in silence for a long while. Kate was halfway mad at Tildy for making her feel so stupid in front of her mother. Just because Tildy knew lots more things than Kate did, she didn't have to be uppity about it. Kate knew things Tildy didn't, too! Hadn't she taught Tildy to knit and to braid her own hair?

They found the first axe mark on the tree close to the river's edge, near where Kate had seen the golden cat. They followed the riverbank, watching the trees.

Tildy was full of talk. Jackson had ridden to Oregon City and had brought back news of the other travelers on their train. "He ran into Mrs. Hammer and Dulcie at the mill," Tildy said with a sidelong glance at Kate.

Kate made a face. Dulcie Hammer was *not* her favorite person. She had never known a girl so snobbish and stuck on herself. Just like her mother. In fact, it was a wonder that Mrs. Hammer had even stooped to hold a conversation with Jackson Thompson. "So how is the queen of the world?" she asked.

Tildy giggled. "Same as always, I guess. Jackson said her curls bounced when she talked and her eyelashes looked as if they were held up on sticks. They rented a place in Oregon City to live until their house is up. Mrs. Hammer told him she couldn't bear to have her children living among wild beasts.

"Peggy Brainard and her family went on across the river into the Tualatin Plains," Tildy went on.

"What about Pansy Parks and her mother?" Kate asked. Mr. Parks had died on the trail. How many times had Kate tried to forget the awful memory of the men piling stones on Mr. Parks's grave and Pansy's desolate face?

"According to Mrs. Hammer, they are still at the mission at Lapwai with Dr. and Mrs. Whitman."

Kate remembered the mission and Dr. Whitman's beautiful blonde wife whose name was Narcissa. Although she didn't have any children of her own, Narcissa Whitman took in orphaned children, both Indian and white, and treated them as her own.

Tildy must have known how sad it made Kate to think about the Parkses because she went on swiftly. "Jackson also talked to Tom Patterson's dad. He said he was coming over to check on his good friend Dan Alexander first chance he got."

Kate giggled along with Tildy. Tom Patterson's dad had once been Dan Alexander's worst enemy. He had even tried to kill him on the trail. But that was before Kate's papa rescued young Tom from drowning during a river crossing.

Kate was feeling better about finding her way by the time they found the fifth tree with a white blaze of exposed wood.

As the trail turned away from the river, the voice of the water faded. The deep layers of pine needles under their feet muffled their footsteps. Now and then a chickaree leaped from their path and skittered away for new shelter, but otherwise it was so silent that it was spooky. Even the twittering of the birds seemed a long way away. The silence made Kate's skin prickle, the way it had when she felt the cougar watching her.

The deeper they went into the woods, the harder it was to walk. They had to climb over fallen limbs that blocked their path. Once they passed under a tree that hummed. When Kate stopped to stare, wide-eyed, Tildy silently pointed upward. A dark slit high on the tree crawled with a great crowd of bees, clambering in and out of the opening. How strange to see bees making honey in the winter. They would never have been able to do that back in Ohio.

"Granny Annie knows how to rob bee trees of their honey," Tildy told Kate. Kate just nodded. Tildy's old friend back in Kentucky seemed to know how to do *everything*. And she had taught a lot of these things to Tildy.

Thorny berry brambles caught at Kate's skirt and the bushes caught at her sleeves and bonnet. "What do you suppose would happen if we wore trousers like the boys do?" she asked Tildy. "It sure would make this easier going."

Tildy chuckled. "I *know* what would happen to me. I'd get one of Paw's famous switchings. I know that because I tried it once back in Kentucky."

Kate glared at her. "You're not going to start fibbing to me again, are you?"

Tildy laughed. "I wish it were a fib. I was on a real tear about then. I got switched twice in two weeks before I settled down."

Kate stared at her, wondering how she would feel if her father ever took a stick to her. The thought made her shiver. "What was the second one for?"

"Riding a pony with my legs on both sides the way the boys do," Tildy said, her tone a little huffy.

"Whatever made you act like that?" Kate asked.

"Whatever makes you ask a question every minute?" Tildy countered in a cross tone. Kate glanced at her and fell silent. When Tildy got prickly like this, Kate knew they were talking about something that hurt Tildy.

Then Tildy spoke again, this time in a low tone. "Since nobody was left at home but boys, I figured I'd be one, too."

Kate was sorry she had asked. That must have been when Tildy's mother "went away." Kate had never asked Tildy why her mother had left. She only knew that thinking about her own mother being gone brought a cold, hard pain to her chest.

In that silence the jays began to shout. Kate looked around, startled. The birds weren't shouting at them. They were too far off in the woods.

"What do you suppose that is?" she whispered to Tildy.

Tildy shook her head, her face a little pale under the dusting of freckles. "Whatever it was has been following us clear since the river," she said softly.

Kate stared at her. "How do you know?"

"I felt it wrinkling along my spine," Tildy said. "I would have told you but I didn't want you to whimper."

Kate would have lashed out at her but a new sound came to them on the breeze, the sound of an axe striking wood.

"Hear that?" she asked Tildy, feeling wonderfully relieved and happy. "Papa and the twins are just up ahead. Let's try to run!"

"I can do better than that," Tildy said. "Shut your ears." The woods exploded with the flutter and shrieks of terrified birds as Tildy whistled the Thompson way, a shrill high note that blasted Kate's ears.

"Halloa there," came Simon's voice, uneven through the trees.

"Now let's run," Tildy said. "We're getting close."

All three of the men were sleek with sweat. Kate's father's red hair, as thick and curly as her own, was pasted against his forehead in dripping ringlets. His blue eyes glistened as he smiled at her. "You girls are as welcome as a spring morning," he said. "I was hollow to my heels."

"And look what your mother sent along," he said, digging into the basket. "She even made lunch for you two rascals to eat with us."

With their lunch eaten, the men stretched out on the pine floor of the forest and shut their eyes. Just when Kate thought her father was drifting off to sleep, he opened one eye to look at her. "You girls better hike on back before Jane starts to worry."

Kate met Tildy's eyes. "Can't we stay with you?" she asked.

His laugh rumbled in his chest. "What kind of nonsense is that? Your mother would be frantic."

"Then maybe we could take Buddy back with us?" Tildy asked. Buddy was stretched out beside Sam.

17

Hearing his name, the dog looked up at Tildy and yawned.

Simon rolled to a sitting position. "What's up?" he asked with a teasing smile. "Don't tell me you got spooked in those big dark woods."

"You'd be spooked, too," Tildy said, "if something followed you all the way from home."

"Maybe your skirt tail?" he asked.

"Stop that," she said. "Something did track us. Kate felt it, too."

Kate's father sat up. "Did you *hear* anything, Kate?" he asked.

"No, Papa," she admitted, "only birds."

"Did you *see* anything?" he asked.

When she shook her head, he frowned at her. "Don't be a baby then or you'll be jumping at shadows the rest of your days." Then he rose to his feet and reached for his axe.

"What about bears?" Tildy asked. "And lions and wolves?"

Simon laughed. "Why would they want two skinny little varmints like you with fat cattle on the farms just north?"

"And Indians," Kate added, more to defend Tildy than anything else.

Kate's father seemed suddenly taller and a little scary as he glared down at her. "Indians are another matter," he said. "You know what I've told you. Stay to the marked trees and keep moving along.

Never mind that the Indians around here are mostly from the mission, you're to have nothing to do with them, hear me?" Kate nodded, drawing a hard tight breath. She always felt scared when he used that tone with her. "Now scat along home and don't dawdle," he said. "These woods are your home from now on."

"Men," Tildy said crossly when she and Kate were out of the men's hearing. Grabbing the empty basket from Kate's hand, she set off running ahead. She didn't slow down until they reached the river's edge, out of the deep shadows of the endless trees and into the light.

But whoever was stalking them was still following back there in the woods. Kate felt it, and knew that Tildy felt it, too, from the way she kept on running even after both of them were out of breath.

3
Molly's Bucket of Stones

The rain began a little while before dawn.

At first the drops only tapped like tiny fingers against the side of the tent next to Kate's head. She snuggled deeper under her buffalo robe and made a face in the darkness. Even the soft beginning raindrops made more noise hitting against the sides of a tent than they had on the shingled roof of their house back home.

Maybe this was because the small tent was worn to almost nothing anyway. It even had leaky places around the patches where her mother had mended it. Kate and her little sister had slept in it all the way from Ohio to Oregon. Her father had better quit walking around and making slashes on trees and get their cabin built before the canvas was completely worn out.

The tent was dirty, too, stained with the dirt of all that territory they had traveled through. When it was damp or rainy, the canvas smelled of cooking meat. Kate knew this was from the spots of grease that had been spilled or splashed on the tent when it stood too near the camp fire. Never mind the reason, the smell made Kate's stomach heave a little.

If Molly didn't always insist on sleeping with her toys, the tent would be plenty big for an eleven-year-old like Kate and for Molly who was only four. Every night Molly dragged in her wooden doll Annabelle and her bucket filled with the stones she had collected along the trail.

Kate groaned silently to herself as the raindrops quickened to a steady, drumming patter. She tried to wiggle down under the covers far enough to shut out the hateful sound and go back to sleep.

She had wiggled too much. Molly, curled beside her under the buffalo robe, stirred awake. "Who's that?" she asked in the barest whisper.

"It's not a who," Kate told her. "It's only rain."

"I'm cold," Molly said, shivering.

"You only *feel* cold," Kate told her, putting her arm around her sister and pulling her close. "Thinking about rain makes me feel cold, too."

Molly nestled against Kate. "You always *feel* warm to me," she mumbled sleepily.

Since it wasn't Molly's fault that she felt cross, Kate didn't answer her. Anyway, it wouldn't do to start Molly talking. Once started, Molly never knew when to quit.

But it was perfectly natural for Kate to feel warm. She was warm because she was alive, that's why.

And she was lucky to *be* alive, too. They all were, what with the rivers and mountains and wolves and rattlesnakes that had been along the trail to Oregon. All that trouble and all that pain just to come to a place where the sky didn't know how to do anything but drop rain! But at least Tildy was here. Without Tildy, Kate knew she couldn't stand it.

The pattering changed to sweeping gusts of rain borne by wind. That did it! How could anyone sleep with all that noise? Kate hated to lie awake in the dark. Her mind always filled up with unhappy rebellious ideas. In the daytime when the sun filtered through the pine trees that surrounded their camp, she could forget how homesick she was. She couldn't push it away at night.

How cozy and easy and warm life had been back in Ohio. And best of all, her brother Porter had been there. Porter had been growing a beard when she last saw him. Would she even recognize him after all this time? Just thinking about Porter made her miss him all over again. And it made her mad all over again, too. After all, he had *chosen* to stay in Missouri and learn to be a doctor instead of coming west to Oregon with the rest of the family.

Kate thought Molly had gone back to sleep when she spoke again. "I don't care what you say," Molly whispered. "I hear somebody breathing."

"*I'm* breathing," Kate told her, not even trying

to keep the crossness out of her voice. "Now go to sleep."

"You don't usually snort," Molly said, tightening her shoulders to press closer to Kate.

Before Kate could answer, she heard it, too, a much heavier breathing than her own, broken now and then by a snort and a kind of labored grunt. This was a wild animal noise, the kind that set Kate's limbs to trembling. The noise sounded very close and just outside their tent.

"Hush," Kate whispered fiercely, hugging Molly tighter. The creature began scratching at the earth by the bottom of the tent, clawing with great harsh nails that scraped like metal on stone.

Kate's heart suddenly thundered in her chest.

A bear. It had to be a bear. No other creature was big enough nor bold enough to try to dig its way into a tent the way their dog Buddy tried to dig ground squirrels out of their holes.

Molly began to cry softly. Her tears soaked into the sleeve of Kate's nightdress, feeling hot for only a moment, before chilling in the cool November air.

A dozen questions and thoughts and horrors tumbled helplessly in Kate's head all in the same moment. She had tried so very hard to quit being a scaredy-cat (as Tildy called her), but she couldn't help it.

But what could she possibly do? She couldn't let that beast, whatever it was, just drag her and Molly out of the tent and maybe eat them. If only the wolfhound Buddy were there! But Simon and Sam had taken the dog off to hunt with them, to try to bring back some game for the Thompson family and the Alexanders to eat.

If there were only some way to get help! She couldn't possibly leave Molly alone, even to go get her father with his gun.

What if the bear had already been at her parents' tent? What if her father didn't have his gun loaded, or was too sound asleep to hit anything if he fired it?

The grunting rose to a snarl as the canvas gave way. The tent ripped open in a long, jagged tear right beside Molly. An icy gust of wind whipped in, and the driving rain that came with it bit into Kate's flesh like needles. As she clung to Molly, gasping for breath, the animal's claws caught the edge of Molly's play bucket and sent it flying, spilling her precious stones all over the robe that covered them.

Molly screamed.

The sound was sudden and loud and piercing. And the noise didn't stop. Molly screamed the way she talked, barely catching her breath between shrieks. From the next tent Kate heard her mother's voice, high with terror, and her father's angry shouts.

But even their voices were drowned out by the cracking of fallen tree limbs and the roar of the animal bellowing as it fled through the woods. Kate's

24

mother was at the flap of the tent at once, calling their names in that high, scared voice.

"Molly!" she called. "Kate! What's wrong? What happened?"

Between her mother's cries and Molly's screams, Kate couldn't get a word out.

"Tell me you're all right," her mother said. "Your father went after it with his gun. Answer me. You are all right. You have to be."

Even with the animal gone, Kate trembled inside from being scared so badly. Her mother's words just hit her wrong. She and Molly were all right if you didn't count being so scared that you hurt all over and had a sudden, hard knot of terror in your stomach.

"*I'm* not all right," Molly wailed, crawling in the rain over the wet buffalo robe. "He spilled every single one of my stones."

For a moment it was silent in the tent except for Molly's angry snuffling. Kate's mother gripped the flap of the tent and swayed against it. In the dimness she was no more than a sagging silhouette.

Then she began to laugh.

Even Molly stopped pawing for her stones to look up at her in disbelief.

Nothing was funny.

But neither was their mother's laughter funny. It was too high and shrill and went on too long. Kate stared at her, scared all over again. She was hysterical. She looked as if she couldn't stop laughing even if she wanted to.

Kate squirmed out from under the robe and leaped up onto her feet. "Mother," she said, not caring that the word sounded almost like an order. Molly, sitting on her knees with her stones around her, looked at Kate and began to sob quietly.

The only way Kate had ever seen anyone's hysteria stopped was by a slap. She couldn't slap her mother; she couldn't. Not for anything. The next time she almost shouted, "Mother!"

Her mother turned to look at her with eyes that didn't even seem to see her. She didn't answer Kate, but she did hear the explosion of gunfire in the distance.

Jane Alexander's laughter stopped as it had begun, halfway through a breath. "We need a light," she whispered, her voice strangely hoarse as she sank to her knees beside Molly. "Go, Kate. Fetch me a light."

Kate hesitated, then let herself out of the tent into the darkness. The woods were alive with sound, the hammer and drip of the rain and the chirped annoyance of disturbed birds. Off somewhere a wildcat screamed, its cry like the wail of an injured child.

The lamp was in the covered wagon. Kate fumbled in the darkness for her father's tinderbox and flints. As she started back toward the tent, her father emerged from the woods. He was running, almost as if something were after him.

"You're not hurt, are you?" he said almost roughly. "Tell me that you're both all right."

Kate nodded.

"Molly, too?" he asked, still fighting for breath.

"And Molly, too," Kate said. "It was a bear then?" Even as she asked, she hoped he would tell her it wasn't.

"It was a bear," he said.

"And you killed him?"

He hesitated a moment. "Between your screaming sister and me, we probably scared him off for good."

Something inside Kate cried out without making a sound. Scaring the bear away wasn't good enough. She would never ever be able to sleep in that tent again with the memory of that clawing and grunting and the harsh ripping of canvas. He might have been drawn by the smell of the salted meat on the canvas, but she didn't care. Not as long as she lived was she ever going to lie down in that awful little tent again.

Her father took the lamp and tinderbox from her hands. The first small hint of color was glowing through the trees to the east as her father set the lamp on the pile of cut wood he and the Thompson twins had piled up as they widened the clearing. Within minutes he had started a glow in his tinderbox. The flames licked up from the spunk. His eyes were in shadow and the lines of his mouth solemn and thoughtful.

"Mother laughed," Kate told him without knowing whether he would realize how scary that had been.

He looked up at her for a long moment. Then his eyes narrowed. "She laughed?" he asked quietly.

Kate nodded. "It was scary," she whispered. He kept looking right into her eyes. He might have been sick for the look of sadness in his eyes. Then he sighed.

"She's stretched as tight as a fiddle string," he said. "We all are. Maybe we should take a day away, maybe in the sun."

The words made Kate's heart leap. For a minute she saw the bright fields of home, the flower-spangled prairie they had left for these dark shaded woods. But he hadn't heard her mother's laughter.

"A day in the sunshine will help," he said, as if repeating the words would make his wish come true.

4
The Outburst

Kate's father held the lantern high as he led her mother and Molly from the torn tent. Her mother walked uncertainly, stumbling a little on the rough ground. If her eyes had not been open, Kate might have thought she was sleeping. No matter how deep a breath Kate drew, she couldn't get enough air into her lungs. Molly held her lips tightly pressed together as she watched her mother's face.

"Fire," Kate's father said to her, wagging his head toward the woodpile. "Try to get a fire going to break this chill."

Grateful for something to do, Kate flew to where the kindling was stored under the wagon to keep it from the rain. She disturbed some small animal when she moved the wood. It squeaked and shot out from between the sticks. Its dark body brushed against Kate's hand before escaping off into the darkness.

Any other time she might have squealed. Instead, she only shivered. She built a small tent of kindling over the wet ashes and laid some smaller sticks over it while her father settled her mother on the stump by the table. He draped a blanket around her, covering her shoulders and hiding her glossy black hair.

The rain had stopped but water still dripped from the trees around them. Along with the distant squawk of jays, Kate heard a sharp, exultant bark. That would be Buddy, coming back with the twins from their hunting expedition. Her heart leaped with hope. Now everything would be all right. Her mother would quit acting strangely, and the horrors of the night would be over for real.

Molly sprang to her feet and would have run toward the sound but her father called her back. "It's full dark yet," he told her. "Wait there by the wagon."

Buddy broke through the trees first, crashing into the small clearing on his long, stiff legs. He swiped Kate's face with his rough, warm tongue and rammed his head against her father in welcome. Simon came next, carrying two guns. Sam followed with a mule deer draped over his shoulders like a lumpy shawl.

Simon stopped at the end of the wagon. His eyes moved swiftly from Kate's mother to the torn tent and then to Kate. His smile wasn't anything like as cheerful as usual. "Up early, aren't you, Kit?" he asked.

Her father answered for her. "We had a visitor just about dawn."

A sense of waiting hung in the air, but her father changed the subject at once. He congratulated the boys on their successful hunt. He said he wished he had coffee ready but it wouldn't be long until he did. From the way he kept talking without mentioning the bear, Kate knew he didn't intend to discuss it with the boys until they were alone.

Even when her father turned to Kate and told her to make coffee, her mother still said nothing. She didn't even greet the boys.

When a faint cloud of steam rose from the pot, Kate threw in the ground coffee. The light of dawn sifted through the trees like colored dust. Kate's father glanced at his wife but spoke to Sam and Simon. "I'm thinking we'll take the day off to ride up to Oregon City," he said.

The twins grinned at each other but Kate's mother didn't stir.

Kate's father went on, his voice brighter. "We can get some tools sharpened at the smithy and look around the town."

"We're at the end of our flour," Kate put in. "Maybe we could get some at the mill."

"No," Kate's mother said quietly.

Kate stared at her mother. Even Kate's father hesitated for a moment. "That's right," he said. "You ladies can buy flour and we might even see sunshine."

"No," Kate's mother said, her tone firmer this time.

"Now, Jane," Dan Alexander said, reaching for her hand.

She pulled away from his hand and rose to her feet, dragging the blanket behind her. "I'm not leaving this place until we have a roof over my children's heads."

"Jane," he said, starting for her.

She backed away, her dark eyes angry on his face. "Don't try to coax me, Dan Alexander. You and your dream. You and your great adventure. I listened and I came. I took the hunger and the thirst and being filthy from the skin out, more an animal than a lady. I lay sleepless listening to wolves howl and worrying over my children. And now I want a house."

Molly, huddled over her doll on the stone, began to sob. Kate couldn't get a breath of air past the pain in her chest. Her father caught her mother by both shoulders and shook her gently.

"Jane, listen to me, Jane."

She shook her head and wouldn't look at him. "Listen! What have I done but listen? And to what end? For rain and fog and wild beasts tearing for my children's flesh in the night. I hate this place, Dan Alexander. I hate it!"

She moved away from her husband. Then she caught her skirt with one hand and ran to climb into the wagon.

Molly's sobs had risen to a wail.

"Quiet that child," her father snapped at Kate.

As Kate turned to Molly, she realized with a surge of relief that Sam and Simon had left. It was scary enough to see her mother so upset. Having other people see it only made it worse. It was also scary to discover that her mother felt the same way about this place that she did. Molly clung to Kate's knees, growing calmer as Kate stroked her head. "You sit with Annabelle," Kate coaxed her. "I'll make you some good bread."

Molly snuffled but obeyed.

Kate took the basin and measured flour into it with the tin cup her mother used. Kate had helped her mother make bread a hundred times. She had made it every day for her father and the twins on the trail when her mother was nursing Molly through scarlet fever. Suddenly she couldn't remember what to do next. Her hand trembled as she stirred the flour, trying to remember.

"Mind you put in soda for it to rise," her father said gruffly. "And salt for the flavor."

She nodded gratefully and worked soda and salt into the flour. Her father sliced thin strips of cured, salted pork, placed the meat carefully into the skillet, and set it on the flames. The fragrant smoke filled Kate's head, making her mouth wet with hunger.

With the crisp meat set aside, Kate laid her flat dough into the greased skillet and put the cover on it. Without being asked, her father helped by heaping red coals on the skillet lid so the top of the bread would cook, too.

The skillet sizzled as the bread rose and browned in the hot bacon fat. Still no sound came from inside the wagon.

Kate knew the bread was good from how high and light it was, but still it stuck in her throat. Molly ate with a miserable sniffle between every bite. Kate's father scowled as he cleaned his plate and helped himself to more.

When he finally spoke, his voice was gruff. "You might set a plate aside for when your mother feels better," he told Kate.

When she glanced at him, he looked away. "Sunshine," he said. "She only needs the brightness of sunshine on her face to feel a world better."

Kate tried to make the strips of brown meat and chunks of bread look pretty on the plate. She found a fresh white cloth and covered the food carefully.

When she was finished, she stared wistfully at the wagon. More than anything she wanted to take the meal to her mother. All her life her mother had served Kate food on a covered plate. When Kate was late getting home, the plate would be waiting on the broad table in the sunny farm kitchen. When Kate was sick in bed, her mother carried a tray all the way upstairs with a mug of foamy milk. She always sat with Kate while she ate. Sometimes in summer when Kate slept late, her mother gave her breakfast out on the porch where the striped bees hummed in the blue morning glories.

More than anything in the whole wide world Kate wanted to serve her mother in that same gentle way, but she was afraid to face her mother's pain again. She stood holding the plate helplessly a long time before setting it on the table.

In the distance that great din of blue jays started again, coming nearer. Her father rose, refilled his coffee cup, and glanced toward the sound. "I didn't even notice when Simon and Sam slipped off," he said. "That must be them coming back." He smiled at Kate, a stiff unnatural smile. "Likely they wanted to tell their pa about getting that fine young deer."

Kate leaned over the skillet, scouring it with angry, rough swipes of the rag. Her father's voice had been light with relief and understanding for the twins. The wagon flap still hid her mother's silence from their view. If her father could be that understanding about the Thompson boys, you would think he could appreciate his own wife's feelings.

But it would be better. It had to be.

Molly dropped her doll with a clatter as she jumped to her feet. "Tildy," she cried, running off at a great rate.

Kate sat back on her heels and looked toward the woods. Sure enough! Tildy was swinging along the path, grinning back at Molly with her bonnet strings dancing loose on her shoulders.

But Tildy wasn't alone. All the Thompson men were coming behind her. The woods rang with their rumbled conversation, and Titus was whistling that bright airy way he did. Tildy's father, Bull Thompson, had a saw hooked over his shoulder, as did Buck, his oldest son. Jackson carried his carpenter tools in a massive wooden box that looked to be too heavy for a single man. Only the twins were not burdened for even Titus and Carl were carrying axes.

When they reached the area by the wagon Kate felt hot tears form in her eyes. The Thompsons made a wall of men, tall and strong and all smiling. She had seen them like this before, when her father was in trouble with Tom Patterson's father. They had come out of the darkness that night and stood behind him and seen him through.

But this trouble was different. If only her mother's unhappiness was something that an army of strong men could make go away.

5
Barter

Well," Kate's father said as the Thompson men stood around the fire. "This is a bit of a gathering." Kate felt the question behind his words. It was almost as if her father was asking what they were doing there.

Bull Thompson laughed and looked around at his brood. "We do fill up a bit of space," he admitted. "But we've come ready to work."

Kate's father flushed. "Don't tell me there's not work enough on your own land, Bull Thompson, because I know better."

Bull nodded. "Work there is and to spare but I came to talk barter."

Kate's mother still hadn't stirred inside the wagon but Kate knew her presence there was on everyone's mind. Before her father could reply, Bull went on.

"There'll be no cabin here until this land is cleared of some trees. Felling trees is dangerous work and no job for a man alone. I figured that my boys and I — "

Kate's father wouldn't even let him finish. "Oh, no," he said swiftly. "It's enough that Simon and Sam have worked for me all this time for the little pittance I can pay them. I'll not take more work from my friends when I have no means to repay them."

"Means," Bull laughed. "If you're talking money, there's less of that here than even back in Kentucky. It's barter I'm talking, our sweat in exchange for skills."

As he spoke, he reached for Tildy and pulled her against him with rough affection. "Tildy here needs help." He grinned at her as he spoke. "I'm not one to complain when a fellow is doing his best, but she'll be the first to admit that she couldn't cook her way out of being hanged."

Tildy giggled and aimed a laughing glance at Kate. Kate smiled back but felt awful about it. If her father had said such a thing about her cooking, she would have sunk right down into her boots. But Tildy had just laughed.

From the way the curtain stirred at the opening of the wagon, Kate knew her mother was listening.

"We didn't so much eat our breakfast this morning as choke it down," Tildy's brother Buck added.

"Mind you," Bull Thompson put in, "it's no blame to the child. No one was ever born knowing womanly arts. But there's none among us that can teach her. We'd like to barter what we do know, how to fell

38

trees and clear land, for what Lady Jane and Kate here can teach our Tildy. Today seemed a good day to start clearing for your cabin, now that your claim is marked."

Kate hid her smile. She loved the way that big rough Bull Thompson called her mother "Lady Jane." Although it was just his way of showing his respect for her, the nickname fitted her perfectly.

Suddenly "Lady Jane" herself was at the opening of the wagon. Her husband stepped over swiftly to help her down. She took his hand but didn't meet his eyes. She stood straight and tall. The strained look had gone from her eyes, and her voice was calm and firm.

"It's an unfair exchange," she told Bull Thompson, "but we'll take it. Maybe the day will come when we can make up the rest."

"But, Jane," Kate's father said, clearly ready to protest.

Jane Alexander's eyes flashed with instant anger. "I've had my fill of fear and terror and beasts in the night. We need a roof over these girls' heads."

Kate felt the same embarrassment that the Thompson men showed by a sudden shuffling of their boots.

"I hope you know what you're getting into," Bull Thompson said, smiling. "I was afraid you wouldn't want to take on such a little savage as Tildy."

Kate's mother looked at him reproachfully and

reached for Tildy. With her arm around Tildy's shoulder, she raised her chin to him. "I'll not have you talk like that about this precious girl."

Kate felt a stab of the same painful jealousy she had felt so often on the trip when her mother stood up for Tildy against Kate herself. Never once had her mother ever snapped at Tildy in anger the way she did at Kate. It wasn't fair. Just because Tildy's mother had gone off and left her, didn't mean she had a right to Kate's mother in her place. Kate would have turned away but her mother called to her. "Kate, I think there's extra coffee already ground. You and Tildy bring us water to make another pot. These men will need to sit and plan their day."

Kate deliberately ignored Tildy all the way down to the bank of the river. Then, as Tildy took one end of the bucket handle, she looked squarely at Kate. "You're mighty touchy this morning."

Kate glared at her. "I didn't say a single word."

"That's what I mean. You have no call to act that way after what I just did. I guess you think it was easy for me to stand there and let Paw say I was good for nothing at all. It wasn't, I'll tell you. But Paw put it to me as a favor to let him talk that way about me."

Kate stared. What kind of a business was this? Why, it was like a plot of some kind. But why? "What else did he say?" she asked, after a minute.

Tildy tugged at the bucket to start back to camp. "Nothing worth repeating."

Kate grabbed the bucket and held it fast. "Stop that. I want to know what else he said."

Tildy groaned. "It's probably not true anyway. It's just what he and the boys think. You don't want to hear it."

"I wouldn't be asking if I didn't want to hear it."

Tildy flushed a deep red and scrubbed her boot on the ground. "All right, Miss Boss," she said. "He said your mother has been worn to a thread by all she's gone through. He said we all needed to pitch in to help her."

Kate set the bucket down and put her arms around her friend. "I've never seen her this upset before," she whispered, fighting tears herself. "But if we can get a cabin up, I'm sure she'll be all right."

Someone was calling from the camp. "Hurry up, you little scamps!" The voice sounded like Simon's.

"Coming!" Tildy shouted, taking hold of the bucket again. "There's more," she told Kate swiftly. "Wait'll you hear the more."

The men had already started their planning. Jackson had put down the rope lines to show the outside dimensions of the cabin. Two large trees and a smaller one stood within his borders.

"Once these three fellows come down, we can level

the earth for the inside floor," Bull was saying as the girls set the bucket by the fire. He squinted up into the branches. "They'll yield enough logs for a fair start. I guess you'll want windows."

Kate's mother, her cheeks rosy again from the fire, looked up in astonishment. "Of course I want windows."

"The next thing you know, she'll be asking for a door," Simon said seriously.

Kate hadn't seen such a smile on her mother's face since the first day they arrived at the claim. "All right, you jokers," she said. "Come get your coffee and quit acting up."

Kate had to wait to hear the "more" until the men finished their coffee. Bull Thompson frowned as he looked again at the big trees. "This is going to be the noisiest place in the valley today and one of the most dangerous," he said. "Those trees are going to come down like thunder, even after the limbs are off." He looked at the girls and then at Jane Alexander. "I'd be a sight more comfortable if we could get you four ladies away from here for the day."

Tildy's eyes danced and she ran her tongue along her lips. Kate still couldn't guess why she was so excited.

"Maybe this would be a good time for the womenfolk to trip up to Oregon City," Buck suggested.

"Tildy's cooked us all out of flour and some of Jackson's tools need work on them."

This, then, was the "more." But Buck Thompson had no way of knowing that Jane Alexander had vowed not to leave the place until a cabin was up.

"If there's calico to be bought, we need some," Bull added. "We're all sick of looking at our Tildy in tatters."

Kate tried to watch her mother's face without being caught at it. She crossed all her fingers for luck and hid her hands under her apron. Her mother *had* to agree to go, she had to!

"They were expecting a ship to come in the day I was last up there," Jackson said. "There might even be mail for some of us."

"Porter," Kate whispered to herself. Could they possibly get a letter from her brother Porter? The very thought exploded with joy in her chest like Independence Day rockets.

Kate's mother started clearing things from the table. "Kate," she said, her voice brisk with command. "You clean up your little sister and do a good job on her hair. I'll get these things put away and be ready in a half hour." Then she paused and looked at her husband with despair. "Oh, Dan," she said. "I'm not even sure I can find the way."

"I'm sending Carl along with the tools we want worked on. He's made that trip enough to know the way," Bull told her. "But you're right about getting an early start. The sooner you get off, the longer a day you'll have."

Molly wriggled under Kate's hairbrush until Tildy insisted on taking over.

Kate was halfway to the wagon when she remembered what Bull Thompson had said about Tildy's dress. She went back and sat down beside Tildy. "Do you remember Fort Laramie?" she asked.

Tildy nodded without taking her eyes off Molly's braid.

"Remember how we dressed up as if we were sisters in those two dresses that Aunt Agatha made me?"

Tildy shot her a hard look. "My dress isn't all that tattered like Paw said."

"Who's talking about your Paw?" Kate asked, in just as sharp a tone as Tildy had used. "I just thought it would be fun to dress the same way again. It would make the trip feel like a party. You could have the blue dress this time if you want."

Tildy concentrated so hard on braiding Molly's hair that Molly squeaked in protest. Tildy was silent so long that Kate decided she was really mad and wasn't ever going to answer. When she finally spoke, her voice was gravelly as always but very low. "I'm nothing like tired of that sunshine yellow one. I'll wear it up to Oregon City if it will make you happy."

44

* * *

Molly rode on the chestnut mare with Kate's mother. Carl, with his tools in saddlebags, rode beside her on a bay horse. Kate and Tildy shared the lazy spotted gelding that was Simon's favorite. By the time they left the clearing, the noise Bull had warned them about had already begun.

The scraping of the saws and the chopping rhythm of axes didn't begin to fade until they reached the path that followed along the Willamette River.

When the path narrowed so that only one horse could pass, Carl pulled ahead and whistled back at the birds that called from the forest. Here and there among the trees, Kate saw the delicate twining of winter roses in full bloom. As if that wasn't enough to make her happy, her mother had begun to hum along with Carl's song.

Kate and Tildy slowed their horse to stare when they reached a settled area. "Where did all these houses come from?" Tildy asked. "I thought we were coming into real wilderness when we came out here."

"Most of it is," Carl called back. "But the fur traders have been up here for a long time. Most of those houses belong to retired workers from the Hudson Bay Company. Since they are mostly French canoers or voyageurs, they call this place the French Prairie."

"I like it," Tildy said, studying the little villages they passed. "Look how neat those houses are in lines with gardens out back, and pigs and cows."

"I could do without that awful smell," Kate said, wishing she could hold her nose and still breathe. Almost every house had a wooden rack beside it. The smoke that wavered up around the red strips of salmon on the racks turned her stomach.

But there was so much to see: the Methodist Mission school, the mill, and an immense waterfall that drowned out their conversation. The water shot into the air in three huge prongs, filling the sky with rainbows and the air with thunderous sound. Carl cantered back to Kate's and Tildy's sides as they reached the outskirts of the town.

"It's big!" Tildy told him.

He nodded. "Biggest town anywhere around." He paused and looked hard at Tildy. "You remember what Paw told you, don't you?"

When Tildy nodded, he left to rejoin Kate's mother up front. "What else did your father tell you?" Kate asked.

"Paw said that you and I were to watch over Molly while we were here."

"She generally hangs onto Mother," Kate reminded her.

Tildy nodded. "He knows that. He just wanted to be sure your mother had plenty of chances to visit around. He says women mourn without the company of other women."

Kate stared at her. "I guess men don't miss other men."

Tildy giggled. "I said that, too. He said he didn't know. With seven brothers when he was a boy and six sons of his own, he hasn't ever had a chance to find out."

6
Oregon City

Kate hadn't really had time to imagine Oregon City until they were there. The town itself was nothing to look at: dirt streets still muddy from the rain and wooden buildings that had never felt a brush of paint, but it was exciting anyway. When they reached the main street, Carl watered the horses and rubbed them down. After tying them to a hitching post, he left for the smithy.

"What do you want to do?" Kate asked her mother.

Jane Alexander's grin was almost impish. "Later I need to buy some things. But first I just want to enjoy walking down a street."

And walk down the street they did, with Molly clinging to her mother's hand and Kate and Tildy following. The men in the town dressed as roughly as they had on the trail and in Fort Laramie, but the women looked splendid in white aprons and starched bonnets just like the women back in Ohio.

Kate and Tildy were staring into a shop window

when Molly squealed. Before Kate could catch her breath, Molly had jerked her hand away from her mother's. She darted toward the road, which was busy with traffic.

A man pushing a wheelbarrow cried a warning to her and tried to get out of her path. As he swerved, the barrow tilted and spilled his cargo of apples onto the road.

"No!" Kate screamed as she darted after Molly with Tildy right behind her.

Molly hadn't even looked back. She was running like a rabbit. She shot past a woman in a shawl carrying a covered basket, and plunged directly into the path of a man on a big dappled horse.

Kate and Tildy both went for Molly at the same time. They reached her at almost the same moment and dived for safety, sliding through rolling apples to reach the side of the street.

Molly's happy cries had turned to screams of terror. The spotted horse whinnied, reared up, and danced wildly on its hind legs while its rider fought to stay on.

Kate's mother was there in seconds, kneeling over the three tangled girls while the rider shouted curses at his horse, at Molly, and at everything else he could put his tongue on.

Kate couldn't figure out where all the people came from so quickly. They were all talking at once and she didn't understand half of the words they used.

She *did* know her knee hurt and she saw a circle of blood widening on Tildy's sleeve. Molly, still wailing, clung to her mother and kept calling out, "Jake! Jake!"

When someone shoved hard against Kate's leg, she looked down. Dulcie Hammer's little brother Jake, who had been Molly's best friend on the trail, was tugging at her skirt, trying to get through.

"Is Molly all right?" he asked. His piping little four-year-old voice was almost tearful.

Kate touched his shoulder. "I think so, Jake. Go see for yourself!" Molly's tears dried instantly at Jake's arrival. They hugged each other, danced around in circles, and seemed unaware that they had caused a public scene. As Kate's mother, her face still pale from her fright, turned toward Kate and Tildy, the crowd around them began to murmur and step back.

Kate looked up to see a woman on an immense white horse approaching at a brisk canter. Kate stared up at her in disbelief. She had never seen a more beautiful woman in her life. Her complexion and hair were dark and she had the bearing of a queen. Her horse was decorated everywhere with bits of silver and strings of clinking bells. The same wonderful ornaments that hung from her bridle reins fringed her long full skirt. Her dress and jacket were made of cotton in brilliant colors: red, purple, and a blue-green as changeable as the sea. As Kate watched, this incredible woman reined in her horse and dropped lightly to the street beside them.

"Astride," Tildy whispered to Kate. "Did you see that? She was riding that horse with her legs on both sides, like a man."

This remarkable woman knelt in the street to look into Molly's face and ask if she was all right. Assured that she was, she rose and looked at Kate and Tildy. "The rescuers," she said. Then, seeing Tildy's bloody sleeve, she frowned. "My dear child, that wound must be tended. And the blood washed out of that pretty yellow dress before it stains."

A fair-haired woman in a blue bonnet that matched her crisp dress nodded cordially to the dark woman but spoke to Kate's mother. "Do come home with me," she said. "I'm just across the way. I'd be more than happy to help." Something about the way she pronounced her words made them sound wonderfully warm and friendly.

The brightly dressed woman turned with a smile like full sunshine. "Dear Mrs. Lauder," she said. "What a good neighbor you are." She turned to Kate's mother. "You couldn't be in better hands than those of Sarah Lauder. Are you new? I don't remember seeing you before."

At Jane's admission that she was, the woman pulled a tiny pouch out of her waistband and handed it to her. "Welcome," she said. "I hope we'll meet again at a happier time, but take these seeds as my welcome gift. They will grow the finest apples you ever dreamed of."

With that, she mounted swiftly and cantered off down the street.

Jake was tugging fiercely on Jane Alexander's skirt. "Please," he said, looking up at her. "Can Molly come home with me to play?"

"Oh, I really think she should stay with me," Kate's mother said, reaching for Molly's hand.

Mrs. Lauder laughed. "Jake lives just across the way from me. You could watch the child from my windows while we tend your little girl."

"Please let Molly play," Jake begged.

"Are you sure your mother won't mind?" Kate's mother asked, looking around. In spite of the excitement, they had seen no sign of Mrs. Hammer.

"She won't even notice," Jake said. "She's off with Dulcie. Anyway, we'll just play in the yard." He pointed down the street to a two-story wooden building with bare windows and a painted sign that read BOARDING HOUSE.

"They'll be fine," Sarah Lauder assured Jane. "But you two stay out of the street! Hear me?"

The smell of delicious soup simmering on the hearth met them at the door of the Lauder kitchen. Mrs. Lauder said, "We'll get acquainted while I take care of this child. Slip out of that pretty dress, dear," she told Tildy. "You can sit by the fire in a blanket while the sleeve dries."

Within minutes, Kate's mother and her hostess were chattering like old friends. After Mrs. Lauder cleaned Tildy's scraped arm and put a poultice on it, she washed the sleeve of the dress and draped it by the fire to dry. By that time the kettle was singing. She insisted they all have some soup. She served this with steaming cups of tea and flat biscuits crusted with salt.

"I know the girls are as curious as I am," Jane Alexander said. "Who was that remarkable woman who gave me the apple seeds?"

Mrs. Lauder laughed. "Gracious. I thought you knew. That's Mrs. McLoughlin, the wife of the Chief Factor for the Hudson Bay Company post at Fort Vancouver. Isn't she a wonder? She and her husband have had nothing but problems about who owns this territory but they still couldn't be nicer to every newcomer."

Kate knew she shouldn't interrupt a grown-up conversation but she couldn't stand it. "Is that the same Mr. McLoughlin who brought flour and supplies to all of us when we were so hungry back on the trail?"

Mrs. Lauder nodded. "It had to be the same. Was this a great, tall man, over six feet, with the carriage of a king?"

When Kate nodded, she went on. "He's saved the lives of more Americans than anyone can count. And not only those he feeds and gives horses to."

"What do you mean by that?" Kate's mother asked.

"The Indians love him for his fairness," Mrs. Lauder said, finally taking a chair. "They call him 'White Eagle' because of that white plume in his black hair. They make no secret that they would have driven out the settlers if John McLoughlin hadn't made it plain that he would protect them."

Kate and Tildy listened with fascination as Mrs. Lauder described the McLoughlin home at the fort, great halls filled with Indian art, huge dinners with a bagpipe playing for the guests. This all sounded like a fairy tale to Kate, but one she could believe after seeing Mrs. McLoughlin.

When Tildy's sleeve was dry to the touch, Jane Alexander rose. "You have been so wonderfully kind," she said. "But we mustn't impose on your time any longer."

"Impose!" Mrs. Lauder said. "You don't know how much I miss company. If you have shopping, I'd be happy to tag along. I *do* know where all the best buys are." Then she laughed. "Not that there are many of those up here in this far territory."

Jake and Molly were still playing happily in the Hammer yard. Mrs. Lauder gave each of them a handful of biscuits and assured Kate's mother that they could keep an eye on the little ones while they did their errands along the street.

By midafternoon Kate and Tildy had looked at

54

everything for sale in the town. Kate's knee ached from her dive after Molly, and Tildy carried her arm as if it were broken. Kate, leaning against a hitching rail with Tildy, watched her mother's face as she stood visiting with one of the women she had met on the trail. She laughed the way she had in the old days and moved her hands gracefully as she talked with Sarah Lauder and her old friend. "Both of our fathers were right," Kate told Tildy. "Mother needed sunshine, like Papa said, but she was also mourning for the company of women."

Kate heard Carl whistling before she saw him. He was back from the smithy with the tools all repaired. He greeted Jane and nodded as she introduced him to her friends. "I've only one more errand," he told her. "They say there's mail in from the states. I'd like to check if we got any."

"Oh, may we go, too?" Kate asked, hoping against hope that there might be something from Porter. At her mother's nod, Kate and Tildy raced off with Carl.

They took a place at the end of a long line of settlers waiting hopefully for word from home. Carl nodded for Kate to go first, but there was nothing in the bag for Alexander.

"You had better luck, son," the agent said, handing Carl two letters, one long one and a short square one, both of which Carl thrust inside his coat.

When they returned, Mrs. Hammer and Dulcie

55

were visiting with Jane. This visit went on too long for Kate's comfort.

"Do plan on coming to stay a while next time," Dulcie's mother said, glancing now and then at Dulcie at her side. "I know Kate and Dulcie would love a good girl chatter together. I was happy to hear from Molly that there is another little girl out there for your Kate to enjoy."

Kate frowned at these words. What in the world did the woman mean? She couldn't be talking about Tildy because Dulcie and Mrs. Hammer had always acted snobbish about Tildy. They looked through her as if she were a pane of glass, and never mentioned her even in conversation unless Dulcie could think of a cause to insult her. "But you are happy out there in the woods?" Mrs. Hammer asked Kate's mother.

Jane Alexander nodded. "And we'll be even happier when we finish a fine cabin like the Thompsons have." Mrs. Hammer's eyebrows rose and dropped without comment as Kate's mother went on. "And that nice Mrs. McLoughlin gave me seeds for a fine start in an apple orchard."

"Dr. John McLoughlin's wife?" Mrs. Hammer asked, not concealing her distaste.

"But she's an Indian," Dulcie said.

The rudeness in her tone was like a dash of ice water. Tildy's face darkened like a storm, and Kate burst out, "She's also the kindest, most beautiful woman I ever saw in my life." She glared at Dulcie's silly little yellow curls and ruffled bonnet.

At Mrs. Hammer's shocked silence, Jane Alexander took Molly by the hand. "Thank you for letting Molly enjoy Jake's company," she said. "I know she had a wonderful time."

Molly *must* have had a wonderful time because she fell asleep at once after Carl lifted her onto the horse with her mother. Cowbells tinkled drowsily as they passed the villages on the French Prairie. Even the sun seemed tired, easing itself steadily downward toward the western mountains as they followed the trail home. As darkness sifted through the trees, the woods became alive with the cries of distant animals. Now and then an owl questioned the shadows or drifted over their heads on wide plumed wings.

The voices of the men sounded through the trees as they left the path to take their own trail. Kate smelled the rich scent of roasting meat before she could even see the camp. "I forgot about the venison," she cried. "I'm starving this very minute."

Her mother laughed softly. "We'll none of us lack appetites tonight, will we? How good it will be to see home." Tildy nudged Kate and grinned at her in the darkness.

Kate gasped and thought of magic. The three trees were gone, leaving a wide open space scraped bare of vegetation. The men had built their cooking fire where the cabin would stand, a grand fire whose flames leaped orange and amber with blue at the base. The burning branches crackled genially. As Sam turned the spit above the flames, the browning meat dripped fragrant juices. They spit and sizzled as they burst to flame.

The men rose to face them as the horses emerged from the woods. Their faces glowed from the light of the giant fire and they were all smiling. One entire side of the clearing was buried under stacks of logs, ready for the start of the building.

"No windows yet," Bull Thompson called to Jane as she stood in amazement, staring into the changed clearing.

"But the door is here," Simon said, sweeping off his hat and bowing low to welcome her in. Jane Alexander's laughter filled the clearing for a long wonderful moment.

Kate's father reached for his wife's hand. "Good luck goes with you. You're just in time for dinner."

Carl disappeared into the woods to return with his fiddle. With dinner over, he leaned against the log pile and played old melodies from home.

"Then it was a successful day?" Kate's father asked her mother.

"Wonderful," she said, her dark eyes on the fading fire. She made little of Molly's dangerous foolishness but told them about the apple seeds and Sarah Lauder's hospitality. "I didn't get the calico you wanted, Bull, because it was too overpriced, fifty cents a yard and the poorest quality ever. Instead, I remembered a length I have in the trunk. It will make Tildy a lovely little dress."

"Oh, no, you don't," Bull Thompson protested. "I'll have none of that."

"Barter," Kate's mother cried, her voice rising until she shouted him down. If he had tried to argue further, he would have been drowned out by the laughter of his sons.

"I got everything else I went for," she went on. "I was just sorry that I didn't have a letter in that packet with news from home."

"Mail," Bull cried, sitting up suddenly. "How about us? Did we fare better?"

"We did indeed," Carl said. He set down his fiddle, pulled a letter from his jacket and handed it to his father.

Kate, tired from the trip and drowsy from her full stomach, listened absently as the letter was read aloud. Then she narrowed her eyes at the fire. What was wrong? Something hadn't happened just right. Then she remembered. Carl had been given two letters. What about the other one?

59

When she looked over at her friend, Tildy was staring at her in a warning way. Then she shook her head, her eyes steady on Kate's. Something about Tildy's expression made Kate not like *this* secret very much at all.

7
Womanly Arts

K ate didn't have to sleep in the torn tent again. Instead, she and Molly slept on pallets in the wagon bed. Since the Thompson men came daily to work on the cabin, Kate usually awakened to find Tildy already there, chattering with Kate's mother.

If clearing the land for the cabin had been like magic, the building itself was double magic, times three. To save time, the men didn't build a real foundation but only piled flat river stones at each corner with some extra ones across the middle. Jackson and Buck were the cleverest with their axes, notching the logs that fitted one over another. The others felled more trees and dragged the split logs to the clearing. Soon the cabin, except for the doorway, was as high as Kate's shoulders all around.

These days flowed as peacefully as the river. With breakfast over, Kate's mother set Kate and Tildy at the table for lessons. The calico for Tildy's dress was pink sprigged with white daisies. When it was washed, dried, and ironed, Jane Alexander got out her muslin pattern pieces to lay on the cloth.

Tildy was so awkward with a needle that she made Kate's fingers itch. It was all she could do to keep from grabbing the work right out of Tildy's hands to make the tiny stitches herself. Often the only sounds in the clearing came from the men, the scrape of saws, the blows of axes, and exchanges of muffled instructions. Tildy was too intent on her work to talk, and chatterbox Molly had become an animal-and-bug watcher. She had learned that the forest creatures only came out when she stayed perfectly quiet. She spent her mornings squatting on the pine needles to watch anything that moved.

Kate and Tildy were free to entertain themselves in the afternoons. Sometimes it took them an hour or more even to think of something new and interesting to do. Since it was nice to get away from the sawing and hammering and thumping, they always left the camp to entertain themselves.

Sometimes they searched the woods for wild strawberries. Although these were not any bigger than a thumbnail, they were as sweet as a whole mouthful of candy. When they found a great many, they took some back to share with Molly.

There were two things Kate didn't like about these free times. The first problem was an old one. Kate couldn't escape that creepy feeling of being watched in the woods. After hearing the bear snort and grunt its way into her tent, she didn't think it could possibly be a bear. A bear would be noisier by far than this silent watcher. Sometimes she wondered if it was the great yellow cat. Or it could even be a wolf, like the ones whose distant howling awakened her at night. Mostly she was just scared. Something was there watching her and Tildy, and it made her skin crawl.

The other problem was that Tildy was suspiciously quiet. Kate understood Tildy not talking when she was sewing or knitting. But when they went out to play, Tildy's silence bothered her. Back on the trail Tildy had turned sad and quiet like this. Later Kate learned that Tildy's father had decided not to come to Oregon with them. He changed his mind, but if something awful like that was hanging over Kate again, she wanted to know about it.

They were throwing sticks into the river pretending they were boats. Kate had tried to make conversation but Tildy just squatted there, throwing sticks and frowning like a thunderstorm rising. Kate finally had enough of that.

"All right, Matilda Thompson," she said, knowing Tildy would really pay attention if she used her whole name. "What's the matter?"

"Who says anything's the matter?" Tildy challenged her.

"I do," Kate said. "You *have* to have something

on your mind to look as sour as last year's pickle."

"Maybe my brains are tired," Tildy said, poking at the riverbank with her stick.

"Tired of thinking about what?" Kate asked.

Tildy stood up suddenly and glared down at Kate. "All right, Miss Nosy," she said angrily. "If you must know, I was thinking about my maw."

Kate caught a quick breath. Tildy never talked about her mother. But here she was, almost the same as bringing the subject up herself.

"I've decided that Maw is crazy," she said.

Kate felt herself go cold. It was bad enough to think something like that without saying it out loud. Somehow saying terrible things made them seem true.

"All right," Tildy said roughly. "Are you going to sit like a stone or do your part of the talking? You could at least ask me why."

Kate's voice almost didn't work. "Why do you think that?" she asked, not able to repeat the other part.

Tildy plumped down again and started poking angrily with the stick. "Look at my brothers. Look how they can do everything in the whole world, like handle cattle, and bring in game, and build cabins. Wouldn't a woman have to be crazy to go off and leave a family like us? I ask you, wouldn't she?"

"Tildy," Kate wailed. "Don't ask me to answer that."

"Then ask yourself what would make *your* mother run off and leave you," Tildy said harshly. "She'd have to be crazy, just the way my maw is."

As she spoke, she leaped up and ran off toward the camp. Kate stared at the water, trying not to think about what Tildy had asked. She couldn't do that any more than she could shake that feeling of being watched. Her skin prickled as the feeling got stronger by the minute.

Then it was too much. She jumped to her feet and turned to run home. She shrieked when she saw Molly standing a few feet away, watching her. "What do you mean, sneaking up on me like that?" Kate cried, her heart thumping.

"I didn't sneak, I was just coming," Molly said. "I came quietly because there was a chickaree."

"Chickadee," Kate corrected her.

Molly shook her head. "That's a bird. This is a squirrel that is named Chickaree. Simon told me."

Kate turned her by the shoulders, aiming her toward home. "Anyway, you're not supposed to come here alone."

"I was looking for the girl."

Kate frowned. "Tildy, you mean?"

Molly shook her head and ran up the path. "The other girl. The one in the woods."

Kate stared after her, then shrugged. Silly little mite. But anyone who talked to stones and a wooden doll could probably make up an imaginary playmate, too.

The log cabin seemed to rise before Kate's eyes. The windows were open to the rain and there wasn't any door, but it looked real. "I wish it was going to be finished for Thanksgiving," Tildy said wistfully as she stopped to thread her needle. Kate winced to see her poke the thread at the little hole a half dozen times and still not get it through.

Kate studied the cabin, imagining it finished. The logs on top were at an angle to support the roof. A great pile of stones from the river's edge waited to be made into a fireplace and the chimney.

"I'm just thankful it's this near done," Kate's mother said, taking Tildy's needle to thread it herself. "Even if they don't get the roof raised by Thanksgiving, I'll be thankful. In the meantime, you girls bring me some fresh water to start beans cooking for supper tonight."

"Beans again!" Kate whispered to Tildy as they set out with the bucket. "We haven't had one good thing to eat since we finished off that deer."

"Men can't hunt and build cabins, too," Tildy said.

"Stop trying to make me feel bad," Kate told her. "Maybe we could find something else for us to eat."

"Roots, maybe?" Tildy asked. "Jackson says the Indians dig roots to eat."

"I like roots," Kate told her. "I like potatoes, and carrots, and onions, and turnips, and peanuts. They all grow underground."

Tildy giggled, then stopped suddenly. "I know. We can catch fish."

"No pole," Kate said.

"Jackson says Indians catch them with their hands," Tildy said. "We could try that."

They left the water bucket by the fire and went back down to the river. The flat rocks by the river looked dry but were so cold against Kate's stomach that they felt wet. Neither of them had any luck at all. The fish wavered past, slithering away from their grasp. Suddenly Tildy grabbed for a big one with both hands. It got away but she slipped in after it, soaking herself from one end to the other. Her fall caused a big wave. It splashed over the rock, drenching Kate from her chin to her knees.

"I'm freezing wet," Kate gasped.

"What do you think I am?" Tildy asked crossly.

When they dragged, dripping, out of the woods, their teeth were chattering. Kate's mother shook her head, looking at them. "Now what have you done? Look at these dresses. You're both soaked. The first one of you that sneezes, you both have to swallow a dose of quinine."

"We were only fishing," Kate explained.

"Oh, really?" Simon asked with that mischievous

grin. "And using yourselves for bait?"

"We wanted to surprise you with a nice fish," Kate told him. "To help out."

"If you really want to help, stay out of mischief," Kate's mother told them. Having started the beans over the fire, she went inside the wagon and got them both a change of clothes to save Tildy a trip back to her own house.

After her mother went into the wagon to sort out some of her stores, Kate and Tildy sat warming themselves by the outside fire. Molly sat beside them, trying to make a skirt for Annabelle out of a rag.

"Honey," Tildy said suddenly.

Kate looked up. "What does that mean?"

"Remember that bee tree we passed? Honey would sure improve plain bread."

"That hive was way high," Kate reminded her. "Anyway, why should the bees let us have their honey?"

"We just need to find a lower honey tree. Granny Annie told me about robbing bee trees."

"I know where bees live," Molly said.

"Where?" Tildy asked.

Molly swung to her feet. "I'll show you." She led them into the woods along a winding path. When they could no longer see the cabin she stopped suddenly. "There," she whispered, pointing to a rotting tree leaning against a large pine.

"Wow," Tildy breathed.

"I hear Mama calling," Molly said as she shot back toward the cabin.

Kate stared at the tree. The opening in the trunk was alive with wriggling, humming, golden bodies. Kate looked at Tildy. "Now what do we do?" she asked.

Tildy frowned. "Granny Annie said something about smoke, and how you should cover yourself up."

"How do we get smoke out here in the woods?"

"Fire fits into buckets," Tildy reminded her. Then she hesitated. "Maybe we should ask your mother first."

"It would be more fun to surprise her," Kate said.

Kate's mother and Molly were both inside the cabin when the girls returned. Kate shoveled coals from the fire into the metal pot with the carrying handle.

"You checking on that supper for your mother?" Kate's father called from where he was pressing clay between the logs of the cabin.

"The beans look fine," Kate called.

"What are we going to scoop the honey up with?" Tildy whispered.

Kate took the dipper from the water pail. "What about coverings?" she asked, beginning to wonder if this was really a good idea.

"We can throw our aprons over our heads," Tildy said.

They carried the pail between them and followed the path to where Molly had stopped. Tildy looked over at Kate. "Mind you don't burn that dress with that hot bucket."

"It's my oldest one," Kate said. "It has patches on its patches. Now what do we do?" Kate whispered, as if the bees were listening.

Tildy tightened her lips into a thin line. "First you put damp leaves on the hot coals to make smoke. When it starts coming out, we count to three and run really fast to the tree. While you hold the smoke under the hole, I'll dip the honey out."

When the damp leaves began to smoke, Tildy said, "One."

Kate covered her head with her apron the way Tildy had.

"Two," Tildy whispered.

As Kate caught a deep breath, Tildy said, "Three," and began to run toward the honey tree.

Kate's feet just wouldn't move fast enough. "Hurry up," Tildy called. "Hurry up!"

Then Kate was there by the opening with her smoking pail. The bees seemed to know what was happening. The humming changed into a wild buzzing. The tiny bees poured from the tree like living smoke. They whined around Kate's head as she knelt with the smoking bucket.

"I can't see for the smoke," Tildy wailed. "The dipper's too big. It won't go in to where the honey is."

The bees didn't seem to know their honey was safe. They zoomed in on Kate's and Tildy's heads, crawling everywhere, stinging every which place.

"Run!" Tildy yelled. "Run for your life!"

The bees streamed after them as they tumbled through the woods. The bee stings came like a rain of burning needles. Kate's face, her wrists, and her hands throbbed and pricked. Her skin was already swelling from the blazing poison.

They were both crying helplessly as they staggered into the clearing. Sam saw them first. "Drop," he yelled. "Get down and roll."

Kate's mother grabbed her with a blanket, and began rolling her over and over on the rough ground. Kate couldn't see anything. She heard the men yelling and cursing and a great deal of slapping and thumps. When Kate could finally peer out, her father was waving a piece of tent canvas over the fire, fanning clouds of smoke toward the wheeling, furious swarm that filled the clearing.

It seemed forever before the humming finally subsided and the last of the bees flew away.

Only Kate's mother, and Molly inside the wagon, had escaped. Jane Alexander stared at the girls, her hands on her hips as if she were very angry. Kate knew better because her mother's mouth was puckered to keep from laughing.

Kate's mother brought the soda jar from her supplies. The soda ran out just as she finished pasting patches of wet powder on all of Tildy's and Kate's stings. Simon went back to the Thompson cabin to bring a fresh supply for his own stings and those of his brothers. Every one of the men had been stung. Jackson looked as if he had grown a hen's egg above his right eye and Carl's ears were swollen to double size.

Tildy looked like a spring calf with the spots of white soda all over her face and arms. Kate's own bites burned, even after being treated by her mother. "The honey was supposed to be a surprise," Kate sobbed. "A Thanksgiving surprise."

"It was a surprise, all right," her mother said, chuckling. "As for Thanksgiving, I'm personally thankful to have survived this day full of your surprises. Any more little escapades like that, and I'll have to keep you too busy to think of mischief."

She leaned forward to lay a hand on each of their shoulders. "That goes for you, too, Tildy Thompson. Any fool can dump herself in a river or stir up a hive of bees. Those are *not* womanly arts."

8
Bird

Not until the morning after the great honey hunt did Kate realize how much that little adventure had cost her. Not only did her face look awful, with swollen lumps that itched and burned, but she had also ruined her dress. It was her oldest dress and was almost worn through in places, but it was the only dress she could play in without her mother asking her to please be careful.

Her mother watched her examine the dress. "Maybe I can fix it," Kate said.

Her mother shook her head. "Don't worry, Kate. What's done is done. It really *is* too worn out to mend. Just put it with the things to wash. I'll cut it up later and save the good strong pieces for something else."

While Kate's father and Jackson and Bull joined the roof sections together, Simon and Sam were chinking the logs. They mixed grass and stones with clay from the riverbank. They added water until it spread without running, rather like cool butter.

Since it looked like fun, Kate and Tildy asked to help. Simon grinned and handed Kate his spreading tool. She spread the chinking between the logs and scraped it flat. She expected him to compliment her because her log looked smoother than his. "How's that?" she asked.

He shook his head. "What happens when it rains?"

"The water just runs straight down."

"Only if you're lucky," he told her. "You have to do it at an angle so that it goes in toward the lower log. That gives the water a head start in running off. If you really want to help, you girls could go bring some more river clay."

Digging river clay was *not* fun. Not only was the thick stuff hard to get up out of the earth, but it was so heavy that Tildy and Kate could hardly carry a half bucket between them. Tildy didn't seem to enjoy it any more than Kate did, because she frowned all the time and didn't talk very much.

After beans again for lunch, Kate and Tildy took off for the river very fast before anyone could ask them to help again. Tildy just sat and glared out over the water until Kate was tired of it.

"I wish you'd say something," Kate told her. "I'm fresh out of ideas for fun, and I'm through trying surprises."

"We've got a job we've been putting off," Tildy told her.

Kate stared at her. "What job is that? If it's more clay, my shoulders already hurt."

Tildy leaned close and whispered. "Ever since we've been in these woods, we've been followed. I'm sick and tired of having my skin crawl because of that critter, whatever it is. I say we trap it."

The very word "trap" made Kate catch her breath. She knew about traps, the heavy metal ones on chains that caught an animal's leg. Then there were pit traps, where the creature dropped into a hole it couldn't get out of. She shivered to think of a great red-eyed, roaring beast clawing to get up from a pit at her. "What if it's a bear?"

Tildy shook her head. "It can't be a bear. A bear would be noisier than whatever this is. I think it's a *human being*." Her words came out more as a breath than a whisper.

"Indian, you mean," Kate said, not liking that idea any better than the bear.

"Not necessarily," Tildy said. "It could be some smart aleck kid whose family has settled around here. Like Tom Patterson, for instance. Their place isn't far up the river from ours."

Tildy was right. Kate's father had gone up to see Mr. Patterson a couple of times since they'd been here. Mr. Patterson raised pigs. Kate's father was set on getting stock, pigs, chickens, and even a milk cow to replace the one they'd lost on the trail. "Say it is Tom Patterson, what would we do if we caught him?"

Tildy giggled. "Maybe we could tie his arms and his legs and carry him back to the house swinging from a tree trunk, the way the men bring in an elk."

"Tildy," Kate wailed. Then she saw it in her mind and couldn't help giggling, too.

"Don't think he wouldn't do that to *us* if he had a chance," Tildy said.

Kate laughed again. "Not to me, he wouldn't. He knows his papa would beat him if he touched me. He's afraid of me since Papa saved his life in that river."

"But he wouldn't be afraid to sneak around and spy on us and try to scare us to death."

"I hate to think of making a trap," Kate said. "I've done my digging for today, thank you."

"How about an ambush?" Tildy asked thoughtfully.

"You mean, just lie in wait for him?"

"Something like that. The trick would be to make him think he was following both of us when it was really only one. Then the other one would grab him."

Buddy barked close at hand and footsteps crunched on the trail. Something moved away swiftly in the woods to the right of them. Whatever it was, it fled in such haste that a limb cracked and the blue jays set up their squalling.

"What was that?" Kate asked.

Tildy leaped to her feet and stared into the woods angrily. "Our watcher," she said crossly. "Whoever is coming for river clay scared him away. I'm sick to death of this, Kate. We're going to get that rascal."

As Simon approached, swinging his bucket and spade, Buddy bounded across the rocks and drank noisily from the river. "Thinking up some more surprises?" Simon asked, grinning at them.

"We learned our lesson about surprises," Kate told him. He walked downriver a few paces and dug his sharpshooter spade into the wet clay. How could it look so easy when he did it, and be so hard when she tried it herself?

As he rose with his buckets full, a couple of low-flying ducks quacked along only a few feet above the river's surface. "We ought to build a duck blind out here," he mused. "A nice roasted duck would make a good change from those beans."

Duck blind! Porter had built a duck blind on the back pond back in Ohio. It hadn't been anything fancy, just a pile of sticks big enough to hide in. She and Tildy could build something like that back in the woods. They could hide there and the watcher couldn't see them. She could hardly wait for Simon to leave so she could tell Tildy.

Buddy decided to stay and fish. He charged out into the water with his jaws snapping. When Simon started back, he whistled for the dog to follow.

"He could stay with us," Kate said.

Simon shook his head. "As soon as Sam finishes his wall, he and your paw are going to take Buddy hunting."

"What about you?" Tildy asked.

Simon grinned at her. "We drew straws and I lost. I have to stay with you little rascals."

"And Lady Jane," Tildy reminded him.

"That's the *easy* part," he teased.

Tildy whistled softly when Kate explained her idea. "Hey! That's great. And it won't be hard work like digging."

Gathering the wood to make the hiding place was harder work than Kate expected. Some of the fallen limbs were so old and brittle that they snapped when Kate tried to pull them along. Sometimes whole trees had fallen, but their limbs just bent instead of breaking off, and she couldn't use them.

Finally Tildy stood up and wiped the back of her hand across her forehead. "I say that's finished because I am tired of doing it."

The blind looked like a beaver dam on land instead of water. Mostly it was just a big cone of sticks with a tiny flat opening to crawl in through.

"Want to go first?" Tildy offered.

When Kate shook her head, Tildy sighed, dropped on her stomach, and wiggled inside. "It's great," she called, her voice muffled by the layers of wood. "Come on in."

Kate squatted to peer into the half darkness. She just knew there were spiders and bugs crawling around on that cleared-off earth. Maybe even ants, the biting kind.

"Are you out there being a scaredy-cat again?" Tildy asked in a disgusted tone.

"Stop that! I'm coming," Kate said. She dropped to her knees to crawl in. It was dim and cool inside. The ceiling was so low that she couldn't sit all the way up straight without her bonnet bumping on the roof. "I can't see out," she complained. She was crammed so close to Tildy that she could hear her friend's heartbeat.

"Here's the window," Tildy whispered, pulling back a wad of weed and grass.

Through it Kate saw the next tree over and a patch of blue sky above the river. Suddenly she was excited all over again. "Now how do we get him to come?" she asked.

"We just sit here and wait," Tildy said. "Then when we see him, we jump out and grab him."

"Jump out?" Kate challenged her. "It took me forever to wiggle in through that little hole."

"You're so smart, you think of how to do it then!" Tildy said.

"It needs another door," Kate decided aloud. "A

bigger one, so we can get out fast. Instead of building it all up, we could just lay one of those big pine branches across it as if it fell there."

"Maybe you're smarter than I thought," Tildy conceded when they had taken out the back side of the blind and laid the branch across it.

Waiting was hard work, too. Kate listened so hard that her ears wanted to close up inside. Every time she wiggled, Tildy glared at her. Warmed by the afternoon sun, the blind became an oven. Outside the birds sang and the river babbled along. Inside, Kate sweated, and itched, and finally got drowsy enough to doze off.

Tildy startled her awake by grabbing her wrist and hissing at her to be silent. Before Kate could move, Tildy had shoved the limb away and was gone. Kate listened a moment, her heart pounding. Something was crashing through the woods. That *had* to be Tildy. Then came a cry she didn't recognize.

Once outside, she didn't see Tildy at first. Then, off to the right she saw a flash of color rising and falling. Tildy was down on the ground, thrashing around on the forest floor and yelling angrily.

"Kate!" Tildy howled. "Help me!"

Kate ran, unheeding, through the brush. Tildy was rolling over and over with a slender girl of about Kate's size. The girl was fighting desperately, trying to claw Tildy's arms from around her waist and wriggling to free herself.

"Don't stand there!" Tildy shouted. "Help me!"

Kate knelt and caught the girl's hand. When the girl tried to pull it away, Kate caught her other hand.

"Be careful," Tildy growled. "She bites!"

Tildy rose and pulled the girl to her feet without letting go of her. With Tildy hugging her around the waist from behind and Kate holding her wrists, the girl was helpless.

Kate's eyes filled with quick tears at her look of terror. The girl had wonderful eyes, slanted a little and as black as night shadow. Her hair was black, too, and hung loose around her shoulders. Her cheeks flamed with color. Her long full dress was made of common muslin and was pulled in at the waist with a belt woven with bright designs. A long strand of olive-colored shells, strung like beads, hung down the front of her blouse. She scowled and tried again to tug herself free of Tildy's grip.

"Let go," she said angrily. "Let Bird go."

Kate was so startled that she almost released her hands. "You speak English!"

"I go to Mission School," she said. "*Please* let Bird go."

"Don't trust her," Tildy said gruffly. "She bites."

"You threw me down," the girl said, glaring back at Tildy.

81

"We're sorry," Kate said.

"I'm sorrier than you are," Tildy said. "I'm the one who got bitten."

"Both of you listen," Kate pleaded. "If we let you go, will you stay and talk and not run away?"

The girl was silent a moment. Then she glared back at Tildy. "I'll talk to you," she told Kate.

"Never trust *anyone* that bites," Tildy warned Kate.

"You can trust Bird," the girl said in a proud way. "I'll talk to you."

Tildy grumbled as Kate released the girl and stepped backward. Bird turned on Tildy instantly. "Why chase me? Why throw me down?"

Tildy's golden eyes widened in amazement. "Look who's full of questions. Why did you spy on us in the woods and follow us everywhere we went?" As she spoke, she rubbed her arm where she had been bitten.

"I just watch," Bird said. "I didn't *hurt* you."

"We felt you watching and it scared us," Kate told her. Then, because this wasn't going sensibly, she did introductions. "This is Tildy Thompson, and I'm Kate Alexander."

Bird nodded, still not smiling. "Mission school teach us to say 'Please to meet you.' What do I say when people throw me down?"

"So why did you watch us?" Kate asked.

Bird lifted her shoulders in a graceful shrug and smiled for the first time. "Mission school girls are all Indian like me. I want to see white girls. Want to see you play."

Tildy stood glaring at her and sucking on her sore arm.

"We don't like being watched like that," Kate told her.

"I only want to play," Bird said.

Kate glanced at Tildy, who was scowling fiercely. Even if Kate trusted Bird, would Tildy get over her anger?

"Maybe we could *try* playing together," Kate suggested, looking at Tildy to see how she felt.

"But no biting," Tildy said gruffly.

"And no throwing me down," Bird came right back.

Kate had been afraid to sit or move since releasing Bird. She had the feeling that the girl might fly away at any moment. "Where do you live?" she asked.

"In village with old one, grandmother," Bird said, pointing to the south and east. "I need to go back now."

Kate didn't know what to say. At least Bird wasn't just running away.

"Maybe I come next day," Bird suggested, looking at Kate. Without waiting for an answer, she turned and ran swiftly away in the woods without another word of good-bye.

"Well, anyway, now we know," Tildy said. "I guess you don't think my arm hurts."

"Be fair, Tildy," Kate said, looking into the dark of the woods after Bird. "How would you fight anyone who came flying out of nowhere to throw you down? You might bite, too."

"Well, maybe," Tildy growled. Then she smiled. "What do you think, Kate? Will she come back? Does 'next day' mean the same as tomorrow?"

"I hope so," Kate said. They were halfway to the cabin when the thought struck her. "Tildy, do you suppose Molly has seen Bird following us? Could that be what she meant when she told Mrs. Hammer about the other girl?"

"You could ask Molly," Tildy suggested.

Kate shook her head. "I don't dare. She might let it out to Papa that I had an Indian friend. You know how he feels about that."

The men had already left for their hunt. Simon came to take Tildy home on a horse Kate hadn't seen before.

"Nice, isn't he?" Simon asked. "I broke him for Mr. Weston, and I'm getting to ride him so he'll get used to a saddle."

When supper was over, Kate's mother smiled over

at her. "Tonight we'll sleep in the cabin," she said. "Since it's all closed in except for the windows and the door, we can really think of it as home."

Kate said nothing, but in her heart she was sure that she would never feel at home in this place. Too much was different. Her memories were too strong. She wasn't sure she could even stand it if she didn't have Tildy.

Sleep was slow to come. They put their pallets inside the sturdy log walls. Simon lay his bedding across the open doorway with his rifle right beside him.

It was damp in the cabin, which smelled like pine pitch and wet river mud. Kate's room back in Ohio had always smelled good. Its winter smell came from the lavender blossoms her mother kept in her dresser drawers. In summer, the scent of flowers came in through the open window. Kate missed the rumble of her father's voice visiting by a late fire. And she hadn't realized how safe and comfortable she felt when she could hear Buddy's restless stalking. She had *never* felt scared in her bedroom back home.

But then she couldn't remember ever being this excited back home, either. Her doubts about playing with Bird had vanished once the Indian girl disappeared into the trees. How wonderful it would be for her and Tildy to have a new friend! She couldn't wait for morning. Would Bird come back and play with her and Tildy? She tingled a little with guilt, thinking about her father's orders to have nothing to do with Indians.

But Bird wasn't *just* an Indian. She was a little girl like Tildy and herself, only more exciting.

9
Playmates

Although the next morning seemed to last forever, Tildy *did* finish the blouse of her new dress. When she tried it on over her other dress, Kate watched her silently. Tildy twisted this way and that trying to see every inch of herself in the hand mirror. Kate had thought she knew Tildy Thompson as well as she knew herself. Yet, just lately, Tildy behaved in ways that astonished her. There with her mirror, Tildy looked as puffed up and pleased with herself as Dulcie Hammer always did.

"You should be very proud of yourself," Kate's mother said, watching her. "The blouse is always the hard part to make. You'll find the skirt goes much more quickly."

"But skirts are so big!" Tildy said, eyeing the two pieces of fabric that had to be gathered and joined to make a long, full skirt.

Jane Alexander laughed. "It's a perfect day to sit and sew," she said. "With the men gone it's nice and quiet."

Kate found it too quiet. She was knitting the second stocking in a pair for her papa. She hated doing the same thing twice. If only the minutes would pass as quickly as the stitches slid onto her needle!

Her mother looked over at her. "You certainly have the jumps this morning, Kate. What's on your mind?"

Kate flushed. "Nothing to speak of," she said. That was really true. Going off to see Bird was on her mind, but she certainly couldn't speak of *that*.

Her mother looked around for Molly. The little girl was off at the edge of the clearing where she had found a mouse hole. She was chattering away to herself about making it into a "real house." She was trying to prop chips of wood over the opening to make a pitched roof.

Leaning close, Kate's mother dropped her voice to a whisper. "You might want to make a gift for your sister's birthday. To think! She'll turn five this coming Sunday."

Tildy chuckled softly to herself.

"What was that for?" Kate asked, not liking Tildy's satisfied tone.

"A secret," Tildy said, making a careful knot in the skirt seam.

"I can keep secrets," Kate told her.

"So can I," Tildy said, grinning. "And I mean to keep this one, too."

Kate glared at her. Why did Tildy have to be so

snippy? "All right for you," she said. "Wait until *I* have a secret." After checking to see that Molly wasn't listening, she whispered to her mother, "What could I make that she'd really like in such a little bit of time?"

"You are such a fast knitter that you could make a little blanket for her doll. Maybe you could even fancy it up with a bit of fringe."

At that, Tildy laughed out loud.

Kate glared at her but said nothing. Maybe she ought to learn some manners along with her womanly arts. "I'd love that. Do we have extra yarn?"

Jane Alexander laughed. "There's no such thing as extra yarn when we're this low on money and so far from a store. But I have some little balls of leftover yarn in the trunk. You could use them up to make a pretty striped blanket."

Kate was glad to put the stocking away and dig in the trunk. Most of the little pieces were dark colors, deep blue, and gray and black, not doll blanket colors at all. After putting these back in the trunk, she looked at what was left: two balls of red and one each of white, light blue, and a nice clear yellow. It looked as if there was even enough red for a stocking.

The wonderful idea came into her head with so much force that she cried, "Oh!" out loud to herself. If she saved the red pieces, she could knit a red Christmas stocking for Molly. She could start collecting little things to put into it right away. Maybe she could find some very special stones to add to Molly's collection. And Jackson had taught her how to make a folding fan with a bunch of small sticks and a single nail. What fun to have a fan for Annabelle!

"Something wrong, honey?" her mother asked without looking around.

Kate tumbled the red yarn back into the trunk and gathered the rest into her apron. "No," she said. "Something is wonderfully right. I just had the most exciting idea ever."

"What's that?" Tildy asked, looking up.

Kate hesitated, remembering how smart-alecky Tildy had been about *her* secret. Two could play at any game. "It's a secret," she said, not caring that her voice sounded haughty.

Tildy's eyes gleamed with suspicion as she stared at Kate. "You haven't any secret at all. You're just trying to get even with me because I have one I won't tell you."

Jane Alexander sighed. "I don't know what's got into you two. You seem determined not to get along this morning. Maybe you need to stretch your legs and work some of this nonsense off. You, Tildy, finish that seam while Kate casts on the stitches to start her blanket. Then you can both run off and play."

Kate grinned at Tildy. Secrets weren't nearly as exciting as going to play with Bird. Tildy must have agreed because she lifted her shoulders tight and winked at Kate before going back to her sewing.

Kate suggested that they walk down to the river on the matted pine needles beside the path. "Maybe if we're quiet enough, we can hear Bird before we see her."

As they reached the last of the trees, Tildy put her hand on Kate's arm and nodded toward the river. A pair of ducks grubbing in the shallows had not heard them coming. The ducks were completely upside down with their pointed tails waggling furiously as they dug for food in the mud of the riverbed. When they saw the girls they quacked astonishment and took off. Their wings punished the air and their wet bodies dripped a fine stream of water. As they veered off toward the opposite bank, a single bright feather fluttered down toward the water, a feather of brilliant blue-green edged with white.

Kate thought of the tiny fan she wanted to make and grabbed a limb. She fished for the feather, trying to poke it toward the shore.

"What do you want that for?" Tildy asked. "The woods are full of dropped feathers."

"Not as pretty as this one," Kate said, squatting to catch it.

"Pretty," Bird said behind them. Startled, Kate almost lost her balance and fell in. Tildy laughed and turned to Bird.

"Where did you come from?" she asked.

Bird smiled and nodded toward the woods.

Bird pointed at Kate's duck feather. "Want more?" she asked.

At Kate's nod, Bird motioned them to follow and set off running through the woods. Bird ran swiftly and silently in her soft leather moccasins. After a few feet, Tildy dropped to the ground, took off her shoes, and started running barefooted after her.

"You'll kill your feet," Kate cried.

Tildy grinned, showing the gap in her teeth. "I almost never wore shoes in Kentucky. My feet will toughen right up."

Kate, pounding along in her boots, was soon left behind. Panting a little from the effort, she scowled. It was just plain rude to run off and leave somebody trailing behind.

They were beyond the sound of the river when Kate saw Bird stop ahead. She pointed upward into the foliage of a huge tree and said, "There."

Bird climbed as swiftly as she had run. Tildy left her shoes on the ground, tied her skirt in a knot in front, and scrambled up the tree after her. Kate was still trying to get a foothold on the first branch when the foliage hid them both completely. The rough bark scratched Kate's hands, and her skirt and apron kept catching on sharp little twigs. What was her mother going to say if she ruined *another* dress?

When an angry crow swooped past her head squalling at her, Kate gave up and tried to drop back to the ground. The limb she held suddenly gave way. She tumbled downward, grabbing wildly to catch herself as she fell. Instead of catching on, she fell all the way to the ground, landing on her behind.

She sat a moment, fighting tears. Her hands hurt, her legs stung where pine needles pricked through her stockings, and she felt like a complete baby.

Bird's face appeared through the leaves above her.

"Are you all right?" she asked.

Kate scowled. "I'm not killed, if that's what you mean. But I'm clawed from here to Sunday and I lost my bonnet."

"Wait," Bird called, disappearing into the foliage. Within moments, Bird appeared on a low limb and dropped lightly to the ground. Tildy, pasted with pine needles and bark but grinning widely, was right behind her.

Bird opened her hand to show a great handful of soft gray feathers that she had taken from a nest in the tree. They seemed to swell with life once she released them from the pressure of her hand.

Kate gasped, "They're beautiful."

Bird grinned. "The owl is not home," she explained. "You can make a headdress now."

Tildy chuckled. "A headdress! What are you going to be chief of?"

Kate glared at her. What had gotten into Tildy? Ever since that trip to Oregon City she had either been silent and secretive or downright mean, as if she had to hit out at Kate every chance she got.

The rest of the afternoon went as badly. They raced along the bank of the river with Kate, in her boots, trailing all the way. She wasn't even sorry when Buddy's sharp bark sounded through the woods. That meant that her father and the twins were back from hunting.

Bird stopped, wide-eyed. "I go home now," she said.

"Where do you live?" Kate asked.

Bird pointed to the south and west. "In village with my people."

"Will we see you next day?" Tildy asked, using Bird's own phrase for "tomorrow."

Bird frowned. "Not sure. I must help old woman. Soon after!"

Kate, with her apron full of downy owl feathers, felt a strange sense of loss as Bird left. She didn't mind that Bird did everything better than she did. That somehow seemed right. And Bird was somehow like a rainbow, appearing and disappearing almost without warning, but always leaving a sense of mystery in her wake.

The men had brought back a goose and a brace of ducks as well as a number of rabbits. "But we saw markings of where there are elk," Simon said. "Wapiti, the Indians call them."

"We'll go back there next week," Kate's father said. "What a Thanksgiving feast that would make!"

The next few days passed swiftly. Tildy finished her dress and moved on to cooking lessons. Kate knitted the doll blanket as swiftly as her mother had predicted. She did it in stripes of blue and yellow. The blanket was so pretty that she just wanted to look at it instead of finishing the tedious fringe.

In the afternoons she and Tildy played, sometimes with Bird and sometimes just the two of them. Often at night Kate lay awake, thinking about Tildy. Was her friend being as difficult as she thought or was she just imagining it? She knew for a fact she was sick of hearing her mother brag about Tildy's sewing and her cooking and what a fast learner she was.

The rain on the Sunday of Molly's birthday didn't dampen the party fun at all. Molly jabbered happily over all her gifts: a new apron from her mother, a low bench from her father, and Kate's wonderful blanket, which Molly wrapped around Annabelle with a cry of joy. All the Thompsons had come to share the ginger cake Kate's mother had made.

"Tildy will make the sweet for our Thanksgiving," Kate's mother said. "She's doing wonders with her lessons."

Carl rose with his fiddle under his arm. "Tildy's not the only one who's been taking lessons," he said. "Come on, Titus, let's have a tune for the birthday girl."

Titus blushed scarlet as he took the fiddle from Carl, nodded at Molly, and began to saw away. Kate recognized the tune of "Yankee Doodle" even with the extra wobbles and squeaks. Everyone cheered but Tildy. To Kate's astonishment, Tildy's face darkened with anger and she stared down at her hands all the time Titus was playing. His brothers called for him to play it again. When he did, everyone sang along with him except Tildy.

But Tildy began hopping on her bench with excitement when Bull Thompson went outside. He came back with his hands hidden behind his back. "You shut your eyes tight, Miss Molly," he said. "And don't peek until I tell you."

Kate gasped as he set the tiny, perfect cradle on the floor, lifted Annabelle, and sat her in it. She had never seen such a beautiful place for a doll to sleep. And no wonder Tildy had laughed when she and her mother had talked about making the blanket. The two gifts went together like hot biscuits and strawberry jam!

"Now!" he cried.

Molly squealed with delight, unable even to talk. "Jackson made it," Bull explained, "but it comes with best regards from the lot of us."

Kate felt Tildy press against her on the bench. "That was the secret I was laughing about the day you started making your blanket," she told Kate. "Now tell me yours."

Kate looked at her. It wouldn't have hurt Tildy to tell Kate about the cradle and let her enjoy waiting to see it. Now she could just wait to see Molly's Christmas stocking when it was through.

"A lot of gall you have!" she cried. "You'll see my secret when it comes out in the open, just like this."

Tildy scooted away on the bench. "All right for you," she whispered. "See if I tell you any of my secrets again *ever*. I know what you're making, anyway. What's so big about an old Indian headdress?"

Kate didn't say anything. It served Tildy right to think she knew so much when she was totally wrong.

Kate glanced up to see her mother watching them with an expression of disapproval. How did her mother always know when she and Tildy were fighting even when she couldn't hear their words? Having just had such a mean thought, Kate couldn't meet her mother's eyes, but looked away.

10
Wild Strawberries

Molly's birthday had fallen on the Sunday before Thanksgiving. Kate couldn't remember two such exciting parties so close to each other. The men had left early on Monday to track down the herd of elk and try to bring one in. "Wish us luck," Kate's father told her mother. "All the settlers have been complaining of the shortage of game. The wolves and the mountain lions and bears are beating all of us to it."

They were only gone a day and a half. When they returned to the cabin a little after midday on Tuesday, they had already dressed their great elk at the Thompson cabin and left a share of the meat there. Kate listened quietly as they described the hunt and the kill. She stared at the huge, pronged antlers Sam had tied to his saddle, and stroked the Wapiti pelt, which was a rich, red-brown in color.

Her father came and put his arm around her shoulder. "Pretty, isn't it, Kate?" he asked, smiling down at her.

She nodded up at him and leaned against his warmth. "How did it look alive?" she asked.

"Like a giant deer," he told her. He lifted his hand and held it flat on top of her head. "Almost as long as a buffalo but built lighter. Your head would just come to his shoulder. Why do you ask?"

She just shrugged. She didn't want to tell him that she liked animals alive — even wild ones — for fear he might laugh at her. Back home in Ohio, he had teased her for hiding in her room while the chickens were being killed and dressed for their table.

He guessed what she was thinking, anyway. "So you still have a heart as soft as rice pudding," he teased. Then he hugged her close. "Never mind, Kate. There are worse faults than a tender heart."

Although both the twins and Kate's mother kept talking about what a grand feast they would have, Kate's father was more excited about his trade. "I bartered half of my share to Patterson for three young pigs," he told Kate. "As soon as I get a shed built, we'll bring them home."

Dawn still streaked the sky when Kate's mother roused her. "Happy Thanksgiving, Kate," her mother said, smiling. "Dress yourself and Molly. This will be a long day."

"Why so early?" Kate asked, yawning.

"Your father has already laid an outside fire to

cook the elk," her mother explained. "We'll have a real feast!"

The Thanksgiving dinner preparations began as soon as breakfast was cleared away. The rest of the meal would be cooked on the hearth inside the cabin and in the special little oven that was built in beside it.

Sam and Simon spelled each other at turning the big heavy spit loaded with meat. Kate started getting hungry the minute the meat began to sizzle slowly over the fire. The smell made her stomach press against her backbone even though she had a good slice of breakfast bread in there. "Stand away from here, would you, Kate?" Simon told her. "If this thing fell you'd be lit like a candle."

She wandered into the cabin with Buddy at her heels. Molly was rocking Annabelle in the corner and her mother was cooking with Tildy. Jane looked over at her and smiled. "Please, Kate, take the dog back outside," she told her. "There's too much going on here to have him underfoot."

After putting Buddy out, Kate put a pan of coffee on to roast. While it browned, she perched on a stool by the table to watch her mother and Tildy work. She didn't mind getting hungrier with every minute. That would only make dinner taste better. She *did* mind the way her mother let Tildy do all of the fun cooking. Tildy got to make two pies of dried apples seasoned with all of Jane Alexander's most precious spices.

Tildy got to pound the cinnamon sticks into a soft brown dust. She got to grate the little egg-shaped nutmeg, being careful not to get her fingers caught in the grater.

The second time Kate's mother walked around Kate's stool to do something, she sniffed the air and grinned at Kate. "Your coffee smells wonderful, Kate. Done to a turn! Now be a love and take the grinder outside to finish it. We don't need to walk a lot of extra miles around you."

Kate pushed her stool back, feeling hurt in spite of her mother's gentle tone. Her mother had always bragged about how good Kate was at helping in the kitchen. Hadn't she earned the right to do some of the fun things, too? Tildy had all the fun. Kate had helped to roast coffee and grind it ever since she could remember. She had *never* gotten to make pies.

But cooking wasn't becoming to Tildy. Her face shone with sweat as she rolled out the dough. Her eyes were wide with fear, as if that silly piece of crust was going to jump up and bite her. Kate knew what Tildy was afraid of. Tildy was proud. She didn't like making mistakes and she didn't like making a fool of herself. Tildy was scared to death that her cooking wouldn't be good enough and her brothers would tease her.

But there wasn't any way that Tildy could make a mistake, Kate thought bitterly. Kate's mother was as gentle as if Tildy were a newborn baby. She practically crooned to her.

"You're doing fine, Tildy," she kept saying. "Roll that dough just a little thinner. Now lift it easy."

Once in a while she gave Tildy an instruction and went out to check the roasting meat but mostly she hung over her young student.

When Kate finished the coffee and put it away in its tin, her mother patted her shoulder. "That's my girl," she said. But she didn't give Kate any exciting cooking chore to do.

It was still *hours* before noon and the big dinner wouldn't be ready before four or five o'clock. With practically the whole day still stretching ahead, Kate was already bored and restless. When she decided she couldn't stand it any longer, she started down the path to the river.

Simon called after her. "Where are you off to?"

"Just fooling around," she told him.

"If you're lucky, you might find some ripe berries," he said. "I never thought to see a ripe strawberry at Thanksgiving until we came to this place."

She kicked stones all the way down to the river. She wasn't about to go alone into the woods to find berries or anything else. Not those great dark woods. When the jays started screaming when she was only halfway down the path, she thought the flying stones had startled them.

Let them scream. She felt like screaming herself. A lot of good it did to have a mother of her own when all she did was pamper Tildy. Not that she was ever *not* nice to Kate, but Kate was getting tired of too much sharing. Never mind how selfish that sounded. A girl only ever got *one* mother. But how could she say that to her mother? How could she talk her into letting Kate make the next sweet — maybe even for Christmas? If she got a chance, she *knew* hers would put Tildy's silly old pies to shame.

When she felt that sense of being watched, she turned, expecting Bird. Instead, the golden cougar lay along that same high branch, watching her. But this time he didn't yawn and go to sleep. Instead, he stared back at her for a long time. She tried not to move to keep from startling him. His eyes were even more golden than Tildy's, and fine hairs rose from the points of his ears, gleaming like strands of silk thread.

Then he changed position, placed his padded feet carefully on the limb, and leaped to a higher branch. Once there, he looked back at Kate before springing like a coiled ribbon into the next tree.

How wonderful it would be to be able to travel from tree to tree through the forest without ever touching the ground. When he leaped from that tree

103

to the next and then to the third one, she followed. She tried to walk soundlessly the way Bird did. When the jays quit their screeching, she felt breathless, as if the woods suddenly belonged to just the two of them, to the golden cat and herself.

Time passed strangely, the way it did when she was dreaming. Insects hummed in the cool air and small birds fluted in the thickets. Kate knew her cat wasn't running away from her because he moved too slowly through the woods. Sometimes he rested on a branch a long time, just staring into the woods before he moved on. Once he sat up quite straight on his branch and groomed himself with his tongue, the way the barn cat back in Ohio used to do.

The cat moved so slowly from tree to tree that Kate, following, didn't worry about getting lost. They couldn't stray far from the river and the path at such a slow pace. She thought about Daniel in the lion's den. Maybe she and the cat could really become friends. He had never looked at all threatening. He couldn't be afraid of her. Indeed, he was as relaxed as any creature could be. Once he even dropped his head onto the limb and closed his eyes to nap.

Kate knew how he felt. She had been awakened early, too. She yawned and sat down with her back against a tree trunk. Tildy was probably still working away back at the cabin, wondering where she was. Kate's eyes flew open at the thought. Maybe her mother would be wondering where she was, too.

She might even be fretting and calling for her. But not yet. It couldn't even be noontime yet. And anyway, Simon would probably tell her that Kate had gone berrying.

The living music of the woods made her drowsy, and she shut her eyes. She leaped awake when a wild, screaming cry sounded not far off. She gasped and tightened her arms against her sides, afraid to move. The cat was gone. The limb where he had been resting was empty and trembling a little in the wind. The wind had risen and the cloud cover deepened. When the sound came again, she leaped to her feet, certain in her heart that this angry and threatening cry was the call of the giant cat.

She tried to stop trembling but couldn't. How could she have done this to herself? She was all alone in the woods she had always feared. But she couldn't be lost. She could find her way back home. She had to. She stood shivering for a long moment, trying to remember which way she had come from. This was of no use. The trees looked the same in all directions, and she was too far from the river to hear its voice. She could not choose the direction to go in.

Back in Ohio, she and her friends had made decisions with choosing games. Now she couldn't even remember how one started. She closed her eyes so tightly that tears squeezed out from beneath her eyelids. And this was no game. What if she chose wrong? Finally she whispered the only rhyme she could remember. "One, two, three, four. Show me where to find the door. Five, six, seven, eight. Run right now or be too late."

She set off through the woods recklessly. Without a path, she couldn't tell whether she was going straight or not. She pushed on anyway, telling herself over and over that she couldn't *really* be lost. She broke through a dense row of underbrush into a clearing. Usually she would have loved to find such a great patch of strawberries bright against their leaves. Instead, she stifled a cry. She hadn't passed any beds of berries while following the cat.

She stared at the berries, turned all the way around and walked back the way she had come. It couldn't be as cold as she felt. She couldn't have walked this far following the golden cat. She *had* to find home. Tired and winded, she leaned against a tree to catch her breath. In that silence, she heard splashing water. The river! If she could only find the river, she could follow it back to the cabin. She had begun to run before she realized the sound was wrong. This was not the sound of the gentle river. This was a rough splashing sound, with other deeper noises mixed in.

Sneaking carefully from one tree to another, she worked toward the sound. At the first glimpse of the water, she gasped. She had reached the river all right, but she was not alone. A great black bear stood waist deep in the stream, slashing at the passing fish with his huge claws. This close, his gasping grunts and growls brought back her terror that night in the tent. She clung to the tree weakly. The river would lead her home. It had to.

As she watched, the bear snagged a large fish and began to devour it. She crept backward through the trees until she was out of sight. Keeping the river to her left she ran through the brush, not caring that it whipped her arms and legs like switches.

Just when she began to panic again, thinking she had gone too far, that somehow this was the wrong way, the wrong river, she heard Buddy's distinctive bark and the shrill whistle that the Thompsons used to signal each other.

"Here I am!" she called, her voice high with relief. "Simon! Sam! Here I am!"

Simon ran breathless to her side. "Run, Sam, and tell the others she's here," he told his brother. For once he wasn't smiling, but was cross with concern. "Where in the world have you been?" he asked. "Your mother is scared to death. Why didn't you answer?"

"I did answer the first I heard you," she told him. "The river's loud."

"You had us all scared, you silly little scamp. We thought you'd gone off and gotten yourself lost." As he spoke, he pulled her close in a big hug.

She wanted to tell about her terror, the cat's

scream, and the bear. She even wanted to admit she *had* gotten herself lost, but remind him that she had found herself, too. A wild tremble of excitement spun in her chest. She *had* made her way home, with the path only a few yards away. What kind of a Thanksgiving would it be for her mother to hear that awful story?

"I'm all right," she told him. "I went farther than I meant to. And I didn't bring any berries, either."

"Who needs berries when we have our Kit?" he said. "Let's get up to the cabin and cool Lady Jane down."

11
Honey Pie

The tiredness Kate had felt during that long walk up the river disappeared as her mother ran down the path toward her. At first neither of them spoke. Jane simply held her while Kate clung to her with both arms tight around her mother's waist. Only when her mother pulled her away to stare into her face, did Kate have to fight tears.

"I'm sorry," Kate cried. "I'm so sorry I worried you."

"It's just that you were gone so long," her mother said. "I wasn't even sure when you left, but it was too long."

"I lost track of time," Kate told her. "I went farther than I meant to. I'm really sorry you worried."

Kate's father had stood a little apart, watching her face. His eyes were narrowed in thought in a way that scared Kate a little. "Did you go by the river or just come back that way?" he asked.

Kate met his glance. How did he know that she really *had* been lost? But he had asked his question carefully so that her answer need not get her mother upset again. She really hadn't lied to her mother. Time truly *had* gotten away from her. But her father's question had to be answered straight out because he knew her so well.

"I went into the woods, then came back to the river to follow it home," she told him.

He stared at her a long moment without smiling. Then he reached for her. When he spoke again, his tone was still grave but his expression had softened. "Do you remember the day that the boys and I blazed this claim with our axes, Kate? And you and Tildy were scared of these woods? Do you remember what I told you then?"

Kate nodded. "I do, Papa. You told me these woods were my home from now on."

His arm was warm around her shoulder. "That's right. Now mind you, I want no more of your scaring your mother like this, Kate. It's thoughtless and selfish and dangerous. On an ordinary day that trick might have earned you bed without supper. But it's Thanksgiving. I'm thankful in part that you've showed me you have your wits about you."

"And I'm thankful she's home so we can eat that good dinner," Simon added, thumping Kate on the shoulder.

Through all this Kate saw Tildy watching her with a puzzled frown. Like Kate's father, Tildy must have guessed that there was more to Kate's story than

110

she had told. Some day she might even tell Tildy all that had happened. But for now, her adventure was too private to try to explain to anyone — even Tildy. Although the afternoon shadows were falling across the clearing, the woods seemed less dark and threatening than they had ever seemed before.

Dinner was finally ready a little after four o'clock. Bull Thompson and every one of the boys came carrying something good to eat. The turnips in the great bowl were golden with butter. Buck carried the hot baked beans, which were flavored with real molasses and a little mustard for the bite. There was honey in a pitcher to go with the fresh hot bread and a great bowl of hazelnuts Jackson had bartered for in town.

How the Thompsons could eat! When Kate's stomach was already complaining about the belt of her apron, they were still refilling their plates and talking.

If she hadn't been so cross with Tildy over taking all of Jane Alexander's attention, Kate would have winked at her. They always giggled about how men said women talked a lot. Women didn't have a chance when men got started. They were worse than Molly and a whole lot louder.

Jackson talked about the big ship up on the river that was due to sail the next day.

"I'd hate to be sailing around Cape Horn in the

111

dead of winter," Kate's father said. "Here in this pleasant place we forget how mean and bitter the winter can be, on both land and sea."

"I understand there are lots of passengers on this one," Jackson put in. "Some of the people who made the trek with us are throwing in the towel. Some of them are planning to get off in California, but most are going all the way back to where they came from."

Jane Alexander shook her head. "How can they do that? After all they went through getting out here."

"Dreams die," Carl said quietly.

Buck laughed. "Mine are alive and well and full of the best meal I've had since Kentucky."

They talked about the constitution that the settlers had drafted the summer before they arrived. "I like the provision that we get this land," Kate's father said. "But I don't like the way we're taxed, never knowing what they'll ask for next."

"I think we need a governor instead of that committee," Buck put in. "We need to keep fighting for revisions and try to get that government back in Washington to clear things up with England."

Kate was so warm and full that she was drowsy when it was finally time to serve Tildy's pies. She yawned as she took the plates outside to rinse them off for the dessert. When she brought them back all dried, she wished she could have *stayed* outside.

Her mother had put both pies right in the middle

of the table. They looked pretty enough, with pale brown crusts over the heaped-up apples. The spices breathed out of the little slits on top, making Kate hungry all over again. Molly was so eager for her piece that she leaned over her plate with her fork clasped in one hand and her spoon in the other.

"Now what do you think of that daughter of yours, Bull Thompson?" Kate's mother asked. "Did you ever see two prettier pies than those two?"

"Not in this life," he said, grinning at his daughter. "Nor did I ever smell anything that set my nose to such a tingling."

When everyone had said something flattering about the pies but Simon, he spoke up. "Somebody once told me that you can't judge a book by its cover. Maybe they said the proof of the pudding was in the eating. I'd like to do a little judging and proofing myself."

Kate's mother laughed, wiped the knife on her apron, and began to cut the pies. They were just as pretty on the inside as they had been on the out. Fat slices of hot, spicy apple slid from under the top crusts as she set the big wedges onto the plates. A fragrant brown juice flowed out, promising a wonderful moistness.

"Nobody tastes it before Lady Jane," Bull reminded them.

Kate's mother flushed, took her seat, cut a careful bite, and lifted it to her lips. The moment she closed her mouth on the pie, her eyes opened wide with astonishment. Tildy looked terrified but Simon, always quick-witted, touched his fork to the juice and tasted it.

"Wait, wait," he cried. "It's not quite ready. Tildy has invented a new treat. This is the world's first honey apple pie. Quick down there, pass along the pitcher and everybody pour freely!"

Kate lifted a bite of the filling to her mouth. It was spicy and warm on her tongue but as sour as a pickle from last year's crock. Tildy had left out the sugar.

Tildy's face began to swell the way it always did when she was about to cry. "Sugar," she wailed. "How could I forget to put in the sugar?"

She leaped up, her stool crashing to the floor behind her. Tears streaming, she flew across the room and out of the door. Kate's mother rose to her feet. "Poor baby," she said. "I'll go to her."

"No," Kate heard herself say as she got up. "Let me."

As she passed her father's chair, he patted her softly and whispered, "Good girl, Kate."

She couldn't answer because her own throat was thickened with tears. A minute before she had been sure that she had *wanted* some embarrassment like this for Tildy. She had been wrong. Her face burned with her friend's shame. Her eyes stung with Tildy's pain, which had mysteriously become her own.

114

After the warmth of the cabin, it felt cool outside, cool and sweet and quiet except for the chirping of the birds. She looked around wildly. Where had Tildy gotten to so fast? She *couldn't* have run home. That would be just too awful. Then she heard Buddy's whine from the direction of the river. She raced down the path, sliding now and then on the loose stones.

Tildy was sitting by the water, curled all over herself as if she wanted to make herself into a ball and disappear. Kate knew how that felt. She had curled up like that the day she discovered that her brother wasn't going to come west with them.

She knelt and clasped her arms tight around Tildy's shoulders. Tildy wailed and jerked her body wildly, trying to push Kate away.

"Don't be silly," Kate told her. "You can't keep me from loving you by shoving me around. That's a great pie, the greatest honey pie in the whole wide world."

Tildy was silent for just a moment. Then her voice was a hoarse whisper. "I just got what I deserved, that's all," she said. "I've been meaner than a badger just lately. I'm really sorry."

Kate tightened her arms around her friend. This was awful. Tildy never ever apologized. She hated saying she was sorry even worse than she disliked being embarrassed or telling people good-bye.

"Stop that!" Kate said, making her voice sound as

cross as she could. "Everybody gets moody some-times."

"But I have a *reason!*" Tildy wailed, starting to cry again.

"Never mind your reasons!" Kate told her. "We need to think *pie*. If we don't nip back up to that cabin about now, those big hungry brothers of yours will have eaten our pieces, too."

Tildy uncovered her eyes and stared at Kate. "They wouldn't dare!"

"You think not?" Kate asked.

Tildy rose and grabbed Kate's arm. Her voice was lower and even more gravelly than usual. "You're a better friend than I am, Kate Alexander."

Kate grinned at her. "It's high time that I beat you at *something*. Let's see if you can beat me racing back to our pie."

12
Tildy's Secret

That next morning, Kate wakened to low, soft voices outside the cabin. She rose on her elbow, confused. The light beyond the window showed only the first brilliant streaks of dawn. The birds had barely begun to sing their early songs. Yet her parents were both gone from their bed.

Something was wrong.

She went to the window in her nightdress, curling her feet against the chill of the floor. At first glance the clearing seemed crowded with people. Then she realized it was only the Thompsons — all of them. Tildy leaned against her father with the other boys ranged behind him. What was the matter? What was going on?

She dressed hastily, pulling her boots onto her icy feet. Molly snuffled and turned over as Kate pushed the door open.

Her mother saw her at once and motioned for her to come. Kate leaned against her mother's warmth and looked at Tildy. Tildy didn't even look back, but stared at the ground as she clung to her father.

"Why don't you girls go down and watch morning come on the river?" Kate's mother asked in a strange, bright tone.

Tildy looked up at her father and he nodded. "That's a good idea," he said.

"I'm already cold," Kate told her mother.

"Then run get two shawls, one for Tildy, too," her mother said. "And mind you don't wake Molly."

Tildy stamped silently along the path beside Kate. She said nothing until they were almost to the river. "They just wanted to get rid of us so they could talk," she said angrily.

"Grown-ups do that a lot," Kate reminded her. Then, in the hope of cheering Tildy up, she added, "Wouldn't it be fun if we could send *them* away when we didn't want them to hear something?"

Tildy only glared at her and plopped down on her favorite broad stone. With her elbows on her knees, she held her chin in her hand and stared out over the water.

Kate tried to think of something to talk about. Tildy *had* to know what was going on, but Kate couldn't make herself ask. She didn't want to say anything about the day before lest Tildy be reminded of her shame about the pie.

Kate chose a flat rock and tried to skip it across the river. It danced only twice before sinking to the bottom.

The longer Kate sat there, the worse she felt. What had begun as confusion was turning into fear. Since being scared made her angry, she felt crosser and crosser at Tildy as the time passed.

The light came swiftly once the sun made it over the snowcapped mountains to the east of them. The moving face of the river glistened and shone. Now and then a fish leaped clear of the water, curling brightly in the light. Still Tildy stared without speaking.

"All right," Kate said finally. "I'm going back up there. They *have* to be through with their talk by now. I might as well be down here with a stone for company."

"I don't feel like talking," Tildy said.

How was she to answer that? Kate said nothing. Would her mother be mad if she went back to the cabin without being called? She was *still* cold. Probably this was from the way Tildy was acting more than from the chill in the air.

"Paw is leaving me with you and your mother today," Tildy said.

"What's so different about that?" Kate asked. "You're almost always here. Anyway, don't you like to stay with us?"

"Sure I do," Tildy said. "It's just that it's different today. What I can't stand is *why* Paw is leaving me. And he isn't even sure when he'll be back for me."

The minutes dragged by. The fish leaped. The

birds sang, and the river chuckled along over its stones. But Tildy *still* didn't explain.

"That's it!" Kate said. She jumped to her feet, totally out of patience. "I don't intend to just sit here and be ignored until I get river rot. I'm going back up to the house. You can come or not as you please."

She took a few steps, then looked back. Tildy had covered her face with her hands. From the jerking rhythm of her shoulders, Kate knew she was crying.

"Tildy," she cried, going back to her. "Whatever is the matter? What's wrong?"

Tildy drew a deep breath that sounded as if it hurt.

"Carl is gone," she said.

Kate stared at her, feeling a sudden ache in her chest.

"Gone?" she asked, almost in a whisper.

Tildy nodded. "Some time in the night."

"What do you mean by gone?" Kate asked. During their long eight months on the trail to Oregon people had died. Their friends announced this in hushed voices by saying they were "gone."

Tildy glared at her as if she had said something stupid. "Gone. Left. Run away. With his clothes and his gun and no note at all. Just gone."

"But where? Where *could* he go from here?"

Tildy stood up. "Any place in the world but here, that's where."

The conversation at the Thanksgiving dinner table echoed in Kate's mind. "Dreams die," Carl had said when they were talking about the settlers who were leaving.

"That's why Paw dumped me on your folks. He and the boys are going to go look for Carl."

The rest of the conversation came back to Kate, too. "The sailing ship," Kate said. "Do they think he could be planning to leave that way?"

Tildy nodded. "That's why we came this early. Jackson says that ships sometimes cast off at dawn before the day's wind rises."

"Do you think he might be on that ship?" Kate asked.

Tildy's voice sounded suddenly tired. "I *know* he's on that ship."

"Tildy," Kate cried. "You *know*? But surely you told your father that."

Tildy shook her head, tears running freely over her freckled cheeks. "I couldn't. I can't." She paused, then grabbed Kate by the arms. "It's so *hard*, Kate," she said. "Why does everything have to be so *hard*? I hate keeping bad secrets. I hate wanting two things at once, and not knowing which one to choose."

Kate picked up a handful of rocks and let them drop slowly through her fingers. How could Tildy's words be so plain and still not make sense to her? But the pain in Tildy's voice pressed against Kate's heart, making it hard even to get words out.

"Would it help to talk about it?" Kate asked. She knew she sounded like her mother. This was the question that Jane Alexander always asked when Kate was sad beyond bearing.

Tildy shook her head, then cleared her throat. "How can talking help? Everybody's so stupid. Why didn't they notice when Carl started doing strange things? He quit singing when he was working. He taught Titus to play that fiddle of his. Why didn't Paw think about that? Carl has never let *anybody* touch that fiddle but himself."

"I didn't think about it, either," Kate admitted. She didn't add that Titus sure didn't have Carl's touch with the bow. But she did understand why Tildy hadn't joined in with the singing when Titus played.

"Somebody should have seen that as a sign," Tildy said. "I kept hoping somebody would notice and talk to Carl. Instead, I just watched it happen. Then last night I had to hear Paw bellowing in the night, looking for his boy."

"Please begin at the beginning," Kate begged. "I just don't understand this at all."

"You were there when it began," Tildy told her. "Remember the day we were at Oregon City and Carl got two letters? You saw that he only gave one of them to Paw."

Kate nodded. She even remembered wondering

122

at the time why Tildy had given her a look that warned her not to mention it.

"That second letter was from Maw," Tildy said.

Kate caught a sharp breath, the way she always did when Tildy spoke of her missing mother.

Once started, the story spilled out in awkward little bursts. Kate couldn't look at Tildy. She couldn't even look at the river because it flowed along so happily. There was no joy in Tildy's tone.

Tildy had recognized the handwriting on that second letter as her mother's. When she asked Carl about it, he had talked to her a long time. Tildy's mother had written to ask Carl to come join her.

"They were always the closest, Maw and Carl," Tildy added.

"Then Carl is going clear back to Kentucky?" Kate asked. The thought of making that terrible trip again chilled her. And even if he went by ship, there was danger. The ship would have to weather the winter storms going around Cape Horn.

Tildy shook her head. "She got to California some way. That's where Carl means to go."

Kate shook her head helplessly. "Tildy," she said. "I can't believe this. How could you know all this and not tell your father?"

Tildy's tears began again with such force that she scrubbed her fists in her eyes angrily. "Carl promised me that if I wouldn't tell, he and Maw would send for me."

She caught her breath and almost wailed the next words. "I miss her, Kate. I miss my mother something awful. I missed her from the very first day I woke up and she was gone. How could I give up the only chance I've ever had to see her?"

It took a second for the full force of what Tildy was saying to hit Kate. She gasped and instant tears flooded her eyes. Tildy go with her mother? But that would mean leaving Kate. The pain of that thought made Kate dizzy. Tildy couldn't go. Didn't she realize how much Kate loved her and depended on her? Life without Tildy? Impossible!

Tildy was looking at her, waiting for some response. Kate wanted to shout, *"You can't leave me! I couldn't bear it,"* but Tildy obviously wasn't even thinking about her, but only of herself.

Kate bit her lip hard, fighting back her own tears. "I guess you couldn't," she finally said. But how could Tildy be so selfish? Even if she didn't think about Kate, what about the others?

Her words sounded ruder than she meant them to. "But what about your father? How could you just let Carl go without giving your father a chance to talk to him, to say good-bye?"

"Paw is bull-headed," Tildy reminded her. "He would have talked Carl out of it. Later they both would have been sorry. And I would have lost my very last hope of seeing Maw."

Kate's mother might have been standing there

beside her for how full and alive she was in Kate's mind. Kate felt her mother's love and gentleness like a warm blanket wrapped around her life. And her mother's spunk, too, the spunk that spiced her words because she cared so much. How selflessly she had nursed poor sick Molly back on the trail. How scared Kate herself had been when her mother got hysterical over the bear in the tent.

"Oh, Tildy," she said softly, using her friend's own words. "That's just too *hard*."

Tildy rose and wiped her face on her soiled apron. "You put that right!" she said. "Now let's go back up there. I know they're gone. Paw aimed to start the first minute he could unload me. He suspects Carl is on the ship, too. He said so."

Halfway up the path, Kate heard Buddy's pleading whine. "That's the way Buddy sounds when he wants something he isn't getting," Kate told Tildy.

Tildy glanced at her with a half smile that wasn't really a smile at all. "Maybe I should learn to make a noise like that. I sure know how it feels."

Buddy was whining from inside the cabin. When Kate started to let him out, her mother shook her head. "He wanted to go off with your father and the others," she explained. "I thought he'd better stay here with us."

"When will they be back?" Kate asked.

"I really don't know," her mother said without meeting her eyes. "You and Tildy wash up and we'll

125

have some breakfast. Let's treat this day like a holiday and just do whatever we want. I have some sewing I've been wanting to get to."

As she spoke, she glanced at Tildy with a look of concern. "You girls can surely think of something that would be fun to do."

For once Kate was glad that Molly was such a hopeless chatterbox. When her sister started explaining *her* plans for the day, neither Kate nor Tildy really had to say anything.

13
Forbidden Places

Kate studied Tildy. What in the world could she do to take her friend's mind off her terrible secret?

Secret! That was the answer. She would tell Tildy *her* secret about Molly's Christmas stocking. Maybe Tildy would even like to help think of things to fill the stocking.

Kate motioned for Tildy to follow her inside the cabin where Molly couldn't hear her.

"I want to tell you my secret," Kate said, leading Tildy to the trunk.

"I'm sick of secrets already," Tildy said sullenly.

"This is a *happy* secret," Kate assured her. When Kate showed her the red yarn and explained her plan, Tildy only frowned more deeply.

"I see right through you, Kate Alexander. You're trying to make me think about something besides Carl."

"It's not as if you could *do* anything about him," Kate reminded her.

Tildy sighed and looked down at the red stocking yarn for a long time. When she looked up, her eyes were narrowed in thought. "Do you remember that tree Bird found with the owl's nest?" she asked.

At Kate's nod, Tildy knelt by Kate. "On the way there I saw a tree with a lot of strange little things under it, maybe nut hulls. We could get some of those. If we could find some really pure clay, we could make her some doll dishes out of it and bake them dry."

"Tildy, that's wonderful," Kate cried, shutting the trunk and jumping to her feet. "What shall we do first?"

"Maybe we should start by finding that tree."

Kate hesitated. "But could we find the tree without Bird's help?"

Tildy nodded. "Sure we could. It wasn't all that far. Anyway, Bird might come help us."

It wasn't easy to convince Kate's mother that they should carry a lunch and not plan on getting back before late afternoon. "I worried about you yesterday enough to last me a while," Kate's mother reminded her.

"This is different," Kate said. "Tildy will be along with me. Anyway, we can tell where we are by Papa's blaze marks on our trees."

"Maybe you should take Buddy along," her mother suggested, still wavering.

"Papa wouldn't like our leaving you and Molly

here all alone," Kate said. "Anyway, we'll come back before the sun starts dropping."

They left from the path by the river as they had with Bird. The woods were cool and fragrant under an overcast sky. Tildy ran off ahead as she had with Bird. As Kate kept fighting her way through the berry brambles after Tildy, she began to feel edgy. Never mind that she had found her way home the day before, she didn't want to be scared like that again. And she didn't remember that the owl tree had been this far from the path.

Tildy didn't seem to have any doubts; she forged ahead as if she knew exactly where she was going. The farther they went, the more concerned Kate grew. The air felt heavier all the time as if it might rain. Worse than that, with the sun behind the clouds, she couldn't tell what direction they were going.

She'd been sincere when she told her mother that they were safe because of the blazed trees. But they hadn't followed the river where they could see them. She wasn't even sure they were still on her father's claim.

There you go, she fussed at herself. You're being a scaredy-cat again, imagining yourself lost!

"Here it is," Tildy cried, "Hurry up!"

Tildy had stopped at a tree that was much shorter than the evergreens around it. The forest floor beneath it was littered with dry leaves and small brown husks.

Kate picked one up. It was shaped like a tiny brown bottle with a fringed neck. "Molly will love these," she cried, stuffing a handful into her apron pocket.

When her pocket was full, she tried to open a husk with her fingernail. Out popped a round brown nut about the size of a cherry. "Hazelnuts," Tildy cried. "We've found a tree of hazelnuts just like those that Jackson got in town. Let's see how many we can find."

Most of the hulls were empty. Kate guessed they had been robbed by the squirrels who were scolding them from the other trees. When Kate had filled her second pocket full of nuts, she looked around. "Where's the owl tree?" she asked Tildy.

Tildy shrugged. "It has to be close around here somewhere because this is the tree I remember."

"But there could be lots of hazel trees in these woods," Kate reminded her.

Before Kate's words were all the way out, Tildy hissed softly and put her finger to her lips.

"What's the matter?" Kate whispered.

Tildy pinched her nose with a finger and a thumb and made a face. Kate smelled the awful odor at that same moment. Just as her eyes began to water from the powerful smell, she saw the little black-and-white animal. It was plodding along only a few yards away. "It smells like a skunk," she whispered.

Tildy glared at her. "But it's all spotted. Skunks have stripes. Anyway, it's not big enough."

"I don't care how it looks," Kate hissed. "Anything that smells like that is a skunk."

The animal stared at them without any sign of fear. In fact, to Kate's astonishment, it turned its back on them. Then it did the most peculiar thing she had ever seen an animal do. It did a perfect handstand the way the boys back home did in the schoolyard when they wanted to show off. There it was, standing on its front feet with its hind legs in the air, showing off.

"Run," Tildy shouted. "It's not only a skunk, it's a crazy one! The next think it will do is bite you and you'll die!"

Tildy could be right. Certainly Kate had never seen any animal do a handstand before. It was scary enough that she scooted backward as fast as she could and found a big tree to hide behind. Tildy was still crashing away in the woods as if the tiny spotted animal were a raging lion.

Suddenly the smell became a hundred times stronger. Kate's stomach heaved from the sharp, acrid stench and she rose to run away before she had to vomit.

Then Tildy yelled. First it was only a howl of surprise. Then her voice came muffled. "Help!" she wailed. "Kate, come quick. Help!"

Kate looked in all directions. She saw no sign of Tildy anywhere. She *did* see a slender column of smoke rising off to her left. At least they weren't all the way lost! But where was Tildy? Although her voice sounded nearer, it seemed to be coming from somewhere below.

The thought scared Kate. Could Tildy have fallen into a pit, or a bear trap? Kate slowed down and kept moving toward Tildy's voice, creeping forward an inch at a time. She came to the edge of an out-cropping where the earth stopped suddenly, and looked down.

Tildy lay on the riverbank several feet below her. When she looked up, her face was twisted with pain. She lay at an odd angle with her left leg tucked under her. And she was crying.

"I didn't see that big drop," she wailed. "I was running without looking. I think I broke my leg."

As Kate scrambled down the embankment, the first uneven patter of rain began. "That's all I *really* need," Tildy said, sniffling. "I always like to have pneumonia with my broken legs."

"You don't *know* that your leg is broken," Kate said, kneeling beside her. "Have you tried to stand up?"

Tildy clung to Kate and tried to get to her feet. When she put her weight down on her left leg, she howled.

"Brace yourself on my back," Kate said. "Let me feel it."

As Kate carefully ran her fingers up her friend's leg, Tildy glared down at her. "What good is that going to do?"

"This is the way Papa checks his horses and cattle," Kate said. Then without thinking, she added, "If there are bones sticking out, they have to be shot."

"Stop that!" Tildy squalled. "Nobody's going to shoot me without a fight."

"You don't have any bones sticking out anyway," Kate said. "And I don't have a gun."

The rain began to fall in a dreary, determined way. Kate's dress was soon soaked and her boots felt slushy.

"What are we going to do?" Tildy wailed. "How am I going to get back home?"

Kate looked down the river and back at the woods. She hadn't the faintest idea where home *was* anymore. That slender pillar of smoke could be coming from their cabin, but the direction seemed totally wrong.

"All right," Kate said. "Which way is north?"

Tildy shook her head, tears welling in her eyes. "You think we're lost?" she said dolefully.

Kate squatted beside her. "We could be," she said. "But there's a cabin pretty close. I saw smoke. I'll have to leave you here alone to go get help."

Tildy shivered and nodded, her lips tight together. "How do you aim to find that cabin?"

"I have to follow the river," Kate said. "Then I'll turn into the woods when I see the smoke again." She didn't add that, unless the river twisted a lot, the smoke could be coming from the other side of the river. Then they would be in trouble!

Tildy tried to smile, then gave it up. "Please hurry," she said, her voice sounding as young as Molly's and a little wavery.

The sky, that had been filled with curdled white clouds, got steadily darker. The woods along the river trilled and chattered with the complaints of birds. Mysterious forest sounds rose over the pattering of the rain. The cracking of tree limbs and high, shrill animal cries raised goose bumps along Kate's arms. She heard a distant scream like the one that had scared her so badly the day before.

Every step she took away from Tildy increased her fear. Back there they had at least been lost together. Now that they were apart, they couldn't even *help* each other. What if she couldn't find the source of that smoke? What if she followed the river too far, past where the pioneers had settled?

The minutes passed like hours. Her wet dress clung to her, and the rain funneled from her bonnet down the back of her neck. She forced herself not to think that animals could be watching her from the deep of the woods. She tried to forget the terrible little story that her Grandmother Morrison had read to her. In the end robins had covered *those* two dead children with wild strawberry leaves.

A great black crow rose screaming from the depth of the woods. Kate jumped and glanced up at it, her heart thundering. Although the bird continued to circle and scream, Kate almost didn't hear it. Instead, she stared at the pale column rising through the rain over the woods. The smoke was behind her! She had passed it! But the fire was on her side of the river.

All that time she had held back her tears. As she plunged into the woods toward the smoke, she began to cry. Her tears mingled with the rain, giving it a salty taste as it reached her mouth.

After a while the trees thinned. The air smelled of burning cedar mingled with a fishy smell, just like the odor of salmon curing racks along the road to Oregon City.

When she reached the edge of the clearing, she caught her breath with a gasp. She hadn't reached a settler cabin. This was an Indian village. The wavering smoke rose from a large central building formed of flat planks. Around it were clustered other smaller buildings, decorated with giant poles carved with the faces of animals and birds.

In spite of the rain a few people were moving about. Two older women in woven hats visited together. A couple of men were working on nets, and a group of young boys were playing. The boys shouted as they shot arrows into the woods, then raced each other to retrieve them. A pack of happy dogs ran yapping back and forth at their heels.

Kate drew back into the shadow of the trees, her heart pounding. What if she got captured and never could get back to Tildy? Every horrible tale she had ever heard about Indians raced through her mind. Maybe if she stayed perfectly still, she could escape without their seeing her.

She had pressed herself tight against a tree when she heard something sing past her into the brush. The boys, shouting and laughing, ran almost straight at her. She panicked and began to run. Blinded by tears of terror, she stumbled wildly through the underbrush, not even caring when the tree branches clawed at her or whipped her face and arms.

The fastest of the boys caught up in a few steps. When he grabbed her arm in a painful grip, her knees softened like warm honey and she cried out in pain.

A taller boy came from the back of the group and shoved the rough hand away. Kate's whole body trembled as she looked up at him. She expected the worst. A tomahawk buried in her skull. Or to be thrown to the ground like a beast.

Instead, he looked at her coldly. "What you do here?" he asked angrily.

"I came for help," she stammered. "My friend is hurt."

His eyes narrowed and he spoke in some other language to his companions. As he glared silently at her, Kate realized he looked like Bird, the same high, rather slanting forehead, slightly angled eyes, and slender, lithe body. He had even talked like Bird. His English was accented and he had left out some words, but she could still understand him.

"Bird?" she asked. "Do you know Bird?"

He looked at her sharply, then waved one of the boys toward the village. "My sister?" he asked, his tone still rough and threatening.

"She is my friend," Kate said.

"We see," he said.

Almost at once Bird came from one of the buildings and ran toward them. An old woman with a walking stick limped along behind her. "Kate," Bird cried. "Why are you here?"

"Tildy is hurt," Kate told her. "Down on the river."

"Trick!" her brother warned her.

Bird shook her head and put her hand on Kate's arm. "My friend. We'll help." As they talked, the old woman approached to stand beside Bird. Her eyes were black coals in a nest of sunburned wrin-

kles. Bird turned and spoke swiftly to her in a pleading voice. As Bird talked, the old woman stared
steadily at Kate's eyes. After a long silence, she
nodded and turned away.

This must have meant she approved. After a quick
exchange, Bird's brother left and returned bearing
a hollowed-out canoe on his head. Once at the river,
Kate sat in its bottom while Bird stood up in the
helm. Her brother paddled in long smooth strokes
with a regular rhythm. The rain had stopped. It gave
way to sunlight that made rainbows bloom on the
other side of the river.

At first Tildy was only a light spot on the riverbank in the distance. Then they were close enough
for Kate to see her clearly. She must have lost all
hope. She lay with her head on her arm staring over
the flowing water.

Bird saw her, too. "Tildy," she called.

Tildy sat up and waved and began to cry again.
Bird's brother knelt by Tildy and lifted her into the
canoe. She winced and made a face as she settled
in. The sunset painted rainbow colors on the river's
face as the canoe sped along. The rhythm of the
paddle in and out of the water was like music to
Kate.

Bird gestured for her brother to draw into the
shore. They were nearly home, at the foot of the
path that led up to the cabin.

When Kate saw the wavering smoke and a light

faintly visible through the trees, she fought back waves of terror.

What would her father say? What would he do? He had told her over and over not to have anything to do with the Indians. She trembled as Bird's brother steered the craft up on the beach and leaped out.

Buddy must have heard them. He barked furiously as he galloped down the path toward the river. Kate heard the excited voices of men right behind him. Her father would be among those men. He was never going to forgive her. *Never!*

14
Miss Porter

The men reached the riverbank just as Bird's brother helped Tildy from the canoe. Kate's father was first, with Bull Thompson and his sons right behind him. Kate knew she would never be able to forget her father's expression. Mostly he looked afraid, but disbelief and anger also twisted his face.

Before her father could find words, Bull Thompson had shouldered past him. Bull strode to the bank and lifted Tildy into his arms. He groaned as he buried her face in his chest, and rested his head on her bonnet. Bird, in the canoe, and her brother on the shore, stood silent, watching.

"Kate," her father roared, his voice heavy with fury.

"Papa," Kate cried. "Papa, listen to me."

As he shouted at her to be silent, Kate's mother pushed past him and ran to Kate. Even with her mother's arms warm around her, Kate couldn't take her eyes from her father's face.

"Please listen to me, Papa," she wailed, trying to

tumble the story out all at once. She *had* to make him understand! Instead, he only yelled at her again, only this time he used her full name, which he only used in anger, "Katherine."

Kate's mother spoke in a firm, clear voice. "Dan Alexander," she said. "You let this child speak her piece."

"Stay out of this, Jane," Kate's father said. "This is between me and my daughter."

Kate felt her mother's body stiffen at his words. "She is *my* daughter, too," she reminded him. "Let her speak."

Kate had seen her mother and father angry at each other before. Back on the trail they had such ill will between them that they didn't even talk to one another, but she had never seen them glare at each other with such blazing fury as this.

She forced herself to speak anyway. "Papa," she said.

He turned to her, his face dark with anger.

"Tildy and I were gathering nuts," she said, her words coming out strained and breathless. "A skunk came, a really strange one. It scared Tildy and she ran without watching where she was going. She fell down a steep bank."

At that he frowned and looked toward Tildy.

"She couldn't walk," Kate told him. "I had to go find help somewhere."

"Kate," her father's tone was threatening. "You

know what I've told you. You know my feelings on this."

"Papa," she wailed. "I didn't have any choice. Tildy couldn't walk. She couldn't even stand up."

Kate heard Tildy start to speak, to try to help her, but she cut Tildy off. This was her own problem. It was just as her father had said. This was just between the two of them. Tildy was safe with her family. He had to see how important that was.

He still hadn't moved, nor had the anger left his face as she went on swiftly. She told about seeing the smoke and following it. Only when she told him about returning with Bird and her brother in the canoe, did her father glance at the two young Indians. His face flushed, and he looked away again quickly as if the sight of them hurt his eyes.

Kate, watching his face, saw something she hadn't seen before — fear. Was it possible that *he* was afraid of Indians? She had always thought he was just afraid for her, but the paleness around his mouth suggested an even deeper fear.

"You know how I feel, Kate," he said, his voice gruff and still angry.

"But Bird and her brother helped us, Papa. They are our friends."

Kate's mother released her and walked swiftly to the edge of the water. She reached out with both hands, one to each of the young people. Although she had no way of knowing that Bird and her brother would understand her words, her thanks couldn't have been more gracious.

Bird nodded solemnly. "Kate is my friend," she said. "Tildy, too."

In the moment of astonished silence that followed, Kate spoke up. "Bird and her brother went to school," she told her father. "You know, the Methodist mission school up by the mill in Oregon City."

The Thompson boys all began to talk at once. Jackson stepped forward, offered Bird's brother his hand, and asked about the handsome canoe. Bull, with Tildy on one arm as if she were a little child, went to pump the boy's hand vigorously.

During this chorus of thanks, Kate's father stood silent. When he finally spoke to Kate, he kept his voice so low that only she could make the words out. "This may have turned out well, Kate, but it changes nothing."

Her father left her side to walk to the side of the boat. He moved stiffly as he offered his hand, first to Bird and then to her brother. His words of thanks were brief and strangely awkward. When he fell silent, Kate's mother invited the young Indians to come up to the cabin.

Bird declined for both of them, explaining that they had promised the "old woman" to return swiftly. Kate watched with the others as the canoe turned and sped off down the river. When her father looked toward Kate, her old fear came back, but only for a moment.

"Nothing is changed, Kate," he repeated. "While I thank God you girls are home safe, you were fortunate this time. You might not be so lucky again."

"Bird is my friend," Kate told him, fearful that he might spoil everything with his stubbornness.

"Let it stop with that," he said. "You know my feelings."

The Thompsons, with Tildy in her father's arms, had started up the path ahead of them. When Kate was sure they couldn't hear her, she looked up at her father.

"Did they find Carl?" she asked, forgetting that the grown-ups had sent her and Tildy away that morning.

He glanced down at her, then tightened his arm around her shoulder. "Carl left on that ship we talked about yesterday. It set sail before dawn, and was well gone before we got there."

Then Carl had gone to join his mother. In time, Tildy would go, too. At the thought, a heaviness settled in Kate's chest. Kate walked the rest of the way up to the cabin in silence. How could she bear losing the best friend she'd had in her whole life? She stumbled a little on the path, made awkward by a grief that was beyond even tears.

* * *

Tildy's leg was not broken, but her ankle was badly sprained. Kate's mother bandaged it firmly, and that night Jackson made her a crutch. Bull Thompson brought her over the next morning to spend the day with Kate and Molly and their mother.

That morning when Kate started back to the cabin with fresh water, Bird stepped from the woods into the path.

"Tildy better?" she asked.

Kate nodded. "Come up to the house. She'd love to see you."

Bird looked doubtful, then shook her head. "Your father won't like," she said.

"He won't mind," Kate said with a little flutter of hope that she was right.

"I bring Tildy a gift," Bird said, putting her fist out and opening it.

Kate almost dropped the bucket. Bird held the smallest basket Kate had ever seen in the palm of her hand. "Oh," she cried, "it's beautiful."

Bird smiled. "You like it?"

"I love it," Kate said. "Oh, come on, Bird. Come see Tildy. It's all right. It really is."

Bird studied her a long moment. "You go first," she said softly. "I come."

When Kate and Bird walked into the clearing, Tildy whooped with joy. She hopped toward them on her crutch like an awkward young robin. Molly came, too, dragging Annabelle behind her.

Kate's father was building a fenced shelter to hold the pigs he had bartered for. He looked up as the girls stopped in the clearing. Kate felt her stomach tighten as he straightened up, stared at them, then started toward them.

Like Kate, Bird watched him come, standing as straight and tight as a drawn bow. As he came into the sunny clearing, he shoved his hat back. "Good morning," he said. The sun glinted on his copper-colored hair and his smile made Kate tremble with relief.

Bird dipped her head and whispered, "Good morning," back.

"Show him your basket," Kate urged.

Bird's great, dark eyes turned to hers, then she held the basket out on her palm as she had to Kate.

Dan Alexander stared at it a moment. Then he leaned to touch it with one finger. He smiled at Bird. "I declare. I've never seen such a basket in my days." He turned and called toward the cabin, "Jane, come out here, will you?"

Kate's mother stood a moment in the open doorway with a startled look in her eyes. Then, wiping her hands on her apron, she came swiftly.

Tildy, leaning on her crutch, winked at Kate as Kate's parents examined and praised the little basket. Bird had made it, she explained, from grasses.

"I bet you couldn't teach anybody like me to do that," Tildy said.

Bird stiffened a little, then smiled. "I can. You can," she said.

That morning passed swiftly. Kate and Bird gathered the grasses and Bird tried to teach Kate and Tildy to weave them. When the sun was high in the sky, Bird rose and thanked them for "good times." She explained that the Old One would worry if she didn't return by noon.

"Is she your grandmother?" Tildy asked.

Bird nodded. "The mother of my mother." Then, after a pause, "My mother go to her ancestors with fever when I was like Molly. I love Old One like mother."

Neither Kate nor Tildy could weave the grasses as smoothly as Bird did, but it was fun to try. Bird didn't come every day but it was always fun when she did.

The nightly rains that drummed against the roof of the warm cabin deepened the snow in the distant mountains. Just looking at those white peaks reminded Kate of Christmases back home in Ohio. The memories didn't come so much in words as in sounds and smells and feelings. Christmas was the jingle of the sleigh bells and the squeak of its runners as she and Porter sped over the frozen roads to their grandmother's house. Christmas was a kitchen rich with the smells of ginger, cinnamon, and sage with Porter holding one end of the chicken wishbone while she pulled. Christmas Eve was Porter carrying her to the barn to see the animals ready to kneel at midnight in honor of the Child.

No day ever passed that Kate didn't think of home. But she had never even dreamed of going back until Carl left. While the thought of Tildy leaving made a hard pain come to her chest, it also made her think. Carl's mother had sent for him. Maybe Porter would send for her. Maybe a letter would come and she could go to live again in a land of painted houses and warm rooms and all the books she could ever read. She wouldn't even mind school.

The thought of leaving the endless rain and the dark of the woods and the fears of the wild creatures was almost too exciting to think about. She decided to write to Porter, to ask him to come for her when Tildy actually left to join her mother. She would explain to him that this had never been home to her and that losing Tildy would take all the joy out of her life. Porter would send for her. She knew he would. After all, her mother and father had Molly. Porter had no one but her. Just like Tildy's mother.

She didn't even tell Tildy these secret thoughts. They were her own to hold in her mind, like the day she had been lost and found herself, like the dreams that came just before she went to sleep. But she did talk to Tildy about Christmas and they both giggled with the excitement of it.

* * *

148

When Kate finished Molly's red stocking she and Tildy filled it with trinkets, including two tiny grass baskets they had made with Bird's help. Kate hid the stocking away in her mother's trunk. Tildy, full of her success with her own dress, cut out a shirt to sew for her father.

Everyone stayed busy. While the twins cleared the Alexander fields for spring planting, Tildy's father and brothers did the same on their own claim.

Kate's father went off to Patterson's and brought back three wonderful little pigs. They were a rich brown with bright eyes and a bouncy kind of strut that made Molly laugh. Their ears were as soft and limp as tiny flapjacks, and they grunted and squealed every minute they were awake.

"That fence could grow to your stomach if you keep lying on it all the time," Tildy told Molly, watching the child hang on the rail to watch the pigs grub in their pen.

Molly stared at her wide-eyed.

Tildy's golden eyes sparkled with mischief. "Didn't I ever tell you about the boy back in Kentucky who was so lazy that he wouldn't get out of bed?"

"All right," Kate cried. "There you go with one of those big fibs. Don't listen to her, Molly. She's only teasing."

"That's all right," Molly said, grinning up at Tildy. "I guess he went walking around with his bed on his

149

back like a snail does with his shell."

Tildy stared at her in astonishment, and shook her head. "You'd better watch this girl," she warned Kate. "She's got the makings of a tall tale teller."

Molly giggled and leaned over the fence again. "Come here, Miss Porter," she called.

Kate froze. "What did you say?"

Molly looked up at her. "Papa said I could name the girl one anything I wanted. We're going to eat the boys so I just call them Bacon and Ham." She pointed a stubby finger at the fattest piglet. "That's Miss Porter. Isn't she beautiful?"

"You can't name a pig after my brother," Kate wailed.

"He's my brother, too!" Molly protested. "I love them both."

Tildy banged her crutch on the ground and hooted with laughter. "Wait'll I tell Simon! Bacon, Ham, and Miss Porter. I love it!"

The rain began earlier than usual that night, before Kate even went to sleep. Across the room, her mother and father sat close together by the dying hearth fire. Without hearing their words, Kate listened to them talk quietly to each other. Once in a while, her mother laughed softly.

As Kate drifted dreamily between waking and sleep, Buddy began to bark in that desperate, threatening way that always chilled her. Over the sound of his barking, she heard the piglets begin to squeal.

She sat up, her heart pounding. Her father was on his feet in an instant. With his gun in hand, he slammed out of the door. Kate flew from her bed and across the room. She could see nothing from the window but gray lines of rain and a sheen on the forest floor where the lamplight fed from the window.

"What's wrong?" she whispered desperately to her mother who had come to her side.

"It's all right," her mother whispered, her hands warm against Kate's back. "Your papa's out there." She gave Kate a little shove. "Now go back to bed, honey, before you wake up Molly!"

The gun went off before Kate's mother could nudge her away from the window. In that blast of light Kate saw a swift, pale shadow leap from the pigpen and escape onto the limb of a nearby tree.

Her father cursed and shot again. Molly flew out of bed and glued herself, screaming, to her mother's knees.

"It's a bear," she howled. "Don't let a bear get Miss Porter."

Kate walked away from the window. That hadn't been any bear. Even that quick glimpse was enough to tell her what it was. The beast her father had shot at was her cat, her golden cat with eyes like Tildy's. What was more and worse, she was *glad* it had escaped safely into the darkness.

Her father came back inside carrying the three piglets in his arms. "We'll keep them in at night until I can build a stronger pen," he told his wife. From his expression Kate knew he expected an argument.

Instead, her mother laughed and folded the fabric from the old tent in a corner near the fire. "You and Molly!" she said. "But the pigs sleep here by the fire and the people in their beds. Hear me, Molly?"

15
The Silent Fiddle

From the first, it was not an ordinary day. It went from tears to laughter and back to tears, leaving Kate spent and heartsick at day's end.

Kate wakened to the sharp scent of lye in the air. Soap. Her mother had saved ashes from every fire since they arrived at this place. Now that she had dripped enough lye from the ashes, she could make soap. Kate knew what she would see when she got outside. Pale, thick soap would be simmering in its black pot over the outside fire. Once in a while her mother would stir the brew and lift it with a spoon to see if it had jelled enough to set when it was poured into trays.

Back in Ohio her mother had made soap out by the chicken yard where hollyhocks grew taller than the fence in summer. When Kate pulled the blossoms and set them on her fingers, they looked like tiny ladies in full, ruffled pink skirts. She closed her eyes and squeezed out the tears that burned behind her eyelids. Were her tears from the strong smell of lye or just from being homesick? She didn't even know herself.

As she snuggled to try to sleep again, a strange grumbling sounded very close. That couldn't be Molly. Molly couldn't possibly make a noise like that. Then, remembering, Kate rose on one elbow to look at the mat by the fire. The pigs were gone and the canvas neatly folded.

The sound came again, definitely from the direction of Molly's cot. Molly was still asleep with her arm draped over Miss Porter's round little body. But the pig was awake and staring back at Kate with bright eyes. She grunted again, softly, as if trying not to wake Molly.

As Molly stirred, Kate threw on her clothes. She went outside without even brushing her hair. "Did you look at Molly?" she asked her mother.

Kate's mother smiled at her through the steam of the simmering soap pot. "I certainly did," she said. "I have to eat my words on that one, don't I?"

"But where are the other two?"

Her mother nodded toward the pen. "Your father put them out when he left. He went to get Jackson's advice on building a solid pig house, one the wild creatures can't get into."

"And he just left that pig in Molly's bed?"

"He didn't want to disturb your sister." She put her arm around Kate's shoulder and grinned. "They do look cute, don't they?"

Kate had to agree, but she also knew Molly. "Don't you think there'll be trouble later?" Kate asked. "After Papa gets a tight pen built?"

"I *know* there will be," her mother agreed. "But I long ago quit taking on fights before they start. Now get your hair done up. Your papa will be back with Tildy any minute and we'll have breakfast."

Kate wriggled her nose. "Everything will smell like soap."

Her mother laughed and lifted a dipper of the smooth, golden brew. "There are more bad smells *without* soap than with. Now scoot!"

Back in the cabin, Molly was sitting on the edge of her bed in her nightdress. She was struggling to tie her bonnet onto the pig. Kate laughed and sat down to help her. Miss Porter squealed and wriggled free the moment the bow was tied.

Her sharp little hooves clicked as she raced for the door. "She knows she looks beautiful," Molly said, tugging on her dress. "She wants to go outside and show off."

Within minutes Kate's father came out of the woods with Buddy and Tildy at his side.

"I guess I expected Jackson, too," Kate's mother said after she had greeted Tildy.

"He told me what I needed to do," Kate's father said, pouring himself a cup of coffee.

"Paw and Buck needed Jackson to help them to-day," Tildy explained. "Titus went off to help a neighbor break some horses that were just driven up from California."

Kate grinned at her. "He'll love that!" she said. Everybody knew how crazy Titus was about horses.

All morning Kate's father and the twins chopped and sawed and hammered, building the new pig house. Molly was finally convinced that her pig couldn't eat wearing the bonnet. After that, she just followed the little animal around, talking to it as it grubbed and rooted for food.

Bird came a little after noon, carrying a basket filled with hard yellow crabapples no bigger than cherries. Jane was thrilled with the apples, which she said would make wonderful jelly. Tildy and Kate were more excited about the basket, which was good-sized and sturdy and made of bent twigs instead of grasses.

When Jane took the basket inside to empty it, Tildy turned swiftly to Bird. "Could I learn to make a big basket like that?" she asked.

"A big one is easier than a little one," Bird told her, shrugging. "Just soak wood to make soft and bend and weave."

Tildy grinned with delight. "That's what I'm going to make your mother for Christmas," she told Kate. "In fact, I'm going to make two; one for your mother and one for mine. Then I'll be ready."

Bird looked puzzled but Kate just looked away. Didn't Tildy even care that it hurt Kate when she

156

talked about going to her mother? Did she even give a thought to how lonely Kate would be when she went away?

"Want berries?" Bird asked.

"They can't still be getting ripe," Kate protested. "It's winter. It's only two weeks until Christmas."

"Ripe," Bird nodded. "Come, I'll show you."

When she was with Bird, Kate was never afraid in the woods. She was still always the last of the three when they set off like this, but that didn't matter. Bird led them to a place where a huge tree had fallen, letting the sun through to a curved knoll of forest floor.

"Glory!" Tildy whispered as she stared at the glowing color. The wild strawberries had sent out curling tendrils in all directions. Here and there among the plants, scarlet strawberries gleamed. Above this carpet of color, a bush of wild roses had burst into full bloom. Kate looked around and smiled to herself. She had been here before, the day she had followed her golden cat.

Bird, her dark eyes as warm on them as her smile, knelt to pick berries with them. "See me count," she said. "One-two-three-Bird!" Kate giggled and did the same, popping every fourth berry into her mouth.

"You don't like berries, Tildy?" Bird asked.

Tildy flushed. "I like them fine," she said. "I just want to take all mine to Paw."

Kate hurt inside at Tildy's tone. How would it be to carry such a secret in your heart day after day, the way Tildy did? How could she watch her father's grief over Carl's leaving while she knew she planned to go, too?

They had started back toward the cabin when Tildy stopped. She whispered, "Sst, listen!" in a fierce tone.

It came again. The shrill piercing Thompson whistle even drowned out the chatter of squirrels and the fluting birds. "That's for me," she said. She handed her berries to Kate, filling Kate's hands to overflowing. "I got to run."

Bird looked at Kate, puzzled. "What's that noise?"

"That's the way Tildy's family signals for each other," Kate said, remembering at least twice on the trail when the Thompsons had called to each other with that whistle, and how happy she had been to hear it on Thanksgiving Day.

"Something wrong?" Bird asked, her dark eyes wide.

"Oh, probably not," Kate said. "They just want her for something." But the sun was still only half-way down the sky. The men should still be working. Kate shivered a little even though no cloud cut off the sun.

Bird told Kate good-bye at the path and disappeared into the woods. Nothing was wrong, Kate told herself over and over as she ran up the path. What could be wrong? Nothing — that's what, absolutely nothing!

But when she could see the clearing, Kate stopped. Her mother stood in the dappled sunlight by the outside fire. She was holding Tildy tight in her arms as she had held Kate herself so many times. Her head was bent so that one cheek rested on Tildy's bare head. Kate knew how that felt, as if a wordless warmth flowed from her mother into her. Tildy's arms were tight around Jane Alexander's waist. Kate knew how *that* felt, too, that if you let go of that loving clasp, the world could crumble away from you.

Simon, his hat in his hand, stood a few feet away, staring off into the woods.

Silence. They were all silent. Only Molly, crooning to her pig wrapped in Annabelle's striped blanket, even seemed alive. The others were like statues in a formal garden.

Kate stopped, her throat aching with fear and pain. She leaned without thinking against the tree at her side and waited. For what? Simon turned. He was taller than Kate's mother by half a head. Though he was lately turned eighteen, he seemed like a great boy as he laid his head against Kate's mother's shoulder and wept.

Kate's tears dripped onto her blouse. That awful thick aching began in her chest. She didn't know the source of their grief. She didn't need to. She shut her eyes against the pain of that scene.

She didn't see or hear her father coming until he was right beside her. He took her by the shoulders and turned her to face the river. She couldn't make the words come out to ask him what awful thing had happened. He answered her unspoken question in a hoarse, pained voice.

"Titus," he said. "He got thrown by one of those wild horses."

"He's *not* dead," Kate whispered fiercely.

He took her in his arms. "God knows I wish he were not." His voice was choked with tears.

"But, Papa," she whispered. "He's not old enough to die. He's only fifteen. He hasn't even got a beard yet."

She felt her father shake his head, but he couldn't say any more for a long time. Then he sighed. "You and Tildy have borne each other up through many trials. Such a time has come again. Be strong."

Molly was humming a lullaby to the poor little piglet upside down in her arms. She didn't keep to the tune any better than Titus had managed to do on the fiddle the only time Kate heard him play.

When Kate's father took her hand to lead her toward the cabin, she remembered the berries she had been carrying. She looked back to see them lying scarlet and wasted on the pine needles beside the path.

* * *

Tildy and Simon and Kate's mother had *stood* like statues in that clearing. The Thompsons *moved* like statues through the two days following.

Kate's father had told her to be strong. She didn't understand what strong meant until she saw the coffin Jackson built for his youngest brother, the grave the twins dug, and the rail fence Bull Thompson put up around the burying place a few yards away from his cabin.

But the price Bull Thompson paid for this strength was written in his face. His eyes were shadowed and the lines around his mouth were deep with pain. He didn't even breathe like a well man. Instead, he drew deep gulps of air that he spent in strangled sobs. He walked differently, in shambling, defeated steps as if he bore the silent weight of the world on his bent shoulders.

He said little, but the words he spoke cut painfully into Kate's memory. "It goes against nature," he told Kate's mother, "that a man should survive his own young."

They knew the preacher Dr. Whitman because he had traveled west with them. Since he was off at a distant mission, Bull asked Kate's father to read the service. "Titus would not like to be spoken over by strangers," he explained.

A crowd of people stood in the uneven shade and paid tribute to Titus Thompson. The Pattersons

161

were there and two other families who had come in the wagon train and settled nearby. The silence Kate had encountered in the clearing stayed between her and Tildy. Tildy would not meet her eyes, nor could Kate find many words to say to her. When Kate did speak, Tildy only nodded or shook her head. Yet Tildy stayed beside Kate all those days. For once it didn't matter whether Tildy talked or not. Kate understood.

When the burial was over, Kate's parents invited all the mourners back to their cabin to share a meal. Once there, the men stood outside talking in hushed whispers. The women, clad in their best dresses and bonnets, unpacked hampers of food they had brought to the service.

"Want to go to the river?" Kate asked Tildy.

When Tildy nodded, they walked together down the path. "I'll come for you when supper is ready," Kate's mother called after them.

They sat on their own rocks with the birds loud behind them. "Paw hung the fiddle up by the hearth," Tildy said after a while. "Maybe he thinks Carl will come back to play on it."

After these quiet words, she startled Kate with the fury in her voice as she turned to her. "I don't care if Carl *never* comes back. He shouldn't have left Paw like that after Paw did all the raising of us. If he comes back, I may even spit on him."

She caught her breath with a sob then went on.

"As for that Belle person, she better not try to send for *me*. I'll tell her what I think, that's what I'll do. I'm never going to leave Paw. He's been left too much already. First that Belle person, then Carl, and now Titus." Her voice broke in a painful gasp.

Even as Kate ached with the pain and anger in Tildy's voice, her heart leaped with guilty joy. Did Tildy mean that? Did she really mean to stay as Kate wished she would? If Tildy didn't go to her mother they could still be happy together the way they always had been. But Tildy's words were altogether shocking. "That Belle person" was Tildy's mother. How could she talk about her in that mean, ugly way? Caught up in the heat of Tildy's words, neither of them heard Kate's mother come down the path.

"You must not speak so ill of your mother, Tildy," Jane said from behind them. "Mothers are people, too, just like anybody else."

Tildy turned and smudged her tears with the palm of her hand. "But she took Carl away," Tildy wailed. "And now look what's happened."

"Did she take Carl away, or only ask him to come?" Jane asked in a voice so soft that the river almost drowned out her words. "The going was Carl's choice, just as our Porter made the choice to stay when we left."

She turned away and then spoke briskly, in her normal tone. "You girls come on up. Supper is ready."

Kate realized that her mother was fighting tears. Tildy must have realized it, too, because she leaped to her feet and caught up with Jane Alexander on the path. They walked together on up to the cabin, with Jane's arm around Tildy. Kate didn't follow until they were all the way there.

16
Winter Roses

The sun shone brilliantly for the three days after Titus's funeral. Without rain there were no rainbows. While the work went on as usual, everyone was different except Molly. Kate's father hardly talked at all, and her mother didn't hum as she worked. Simon still smiled with his lips, but he didn't tease in the old way.

Kate didn't want to cry when she told Bird about Titus, but she couldn't help it. Bird stood completely still for a long time with her head bent. After only a little while she made an excuse to go back to her village.

Kate finished knitting the yellow stockings she had started for Tildy's Christmas gift. When Tildy was with Kate, she hardly talked at all, but only bent solemnly over the Christmas shirt she was making for her father.

Kate's father finished the "bearproof" pig house. That night after supper, he told Molly that Miss Porter would have to start sleeping with her brothers outside. The words were barely out of his mouth before Molly started to wail.

"Come now, Molly," her father said. "It isn't like you to make a fuss. The pig sleeps outside and I want to hear no more about it." With that, he lifted the piglet from Molly's arms and carried her outside.

Kate stared in amazement. Molly didn't even cling to the pig or cry. She just set her face in a hard line and glared at his back as he left.

Dinner was quiet with Molly only pushing her food around and not eating. Since her parents pretended not to notice, Kate did, too. That night they went to bed as usual, and Kate drifted off to the sound of her parents talking together in that cozy way by the fire. It was barely light when she heard her father roar. "Where's Molly?"

Kate sat up in the half darkness. Sure enough, Molly's pallet was empty and her heavy quilt was gone, too.

"Where do *you* think she is?" Kate's mother asked him.

"What kind of an unnatural mother are you?" he roared. "Your child is gone in the night and you play with questions?"

When Jane only looked at him, he spoke again, his tone unbelieving. "She can't be out there in that pigpen," he insisted. "She's never been one for mischief like Porter and Kate have been."

"I'd look before I'd be too sure," Kate's mother said quietly.

He glared at her as he slammed out the door. He was back in minutes carrying Molly. She seemed to be all legs and arms, screaming and kicking like a giant spider in a white nightdress.

"Miss Porter," she shouted, flailing at him with her fists. "Let me down! I want my pig!"

"Molly," Kate's mother called as she took her from her father's arms. "We need to talk about this." When she took the child on her lap, Molly stopped screaming but she glared fiercely at her father.

"There's nothing to talk about," Kate's father said. "The pig is *not* going to sleep in the house, and Molly is *not* going to sleep in the pigpen."

Molly let out a wail that her mother hushed quickly. "What about sleeping with your doll Annabelle?" her mother asked. "You've always done that before."

"Annabelle is cold," Molly wailed. "Miss Porter is alive like me. And she's little like me, too."

Kate's mother frowned a moment, then looked up at her husband. "Maybe we could compromise."

"No," Kate's father said firmly.

Kate's mother just went on talking. "Molly doesn't have playmates like Kate has. She doesn't even have a kitten the way she did back home. How about we let the pig — "

"No," Kate's father broke in, louder this time.

Kate's mother raised her voice a little. "How about we let the pig sleep with Molly as long as Molly can carry her?" she asked, ignoring his black expression.

Molly stared at her. "She's not heavy."

"But she will be," her mother said. "And when she is, she can sleep outside with the others. Is that a good idea?"

"Jane," Kate's father protested.

She smiled at him. "Dan, pigs grow a lot faster than little girls do," she reminded him.

Kate knew he had given up when he turned and went out of the cabin without even looking back.

That Friday when Jackson rode to Oregon City for supplies, he brought them three letters. Two were addressed to Jane Alexander and one was for Kate. Kate's heart leaped. Porter. She was sure her letter was going to be from Porter until she saw the name "Amy Lyons" written on the envelope. Although Amy had been her best friend back in Ohio, Kate just held the letter, waiting for her disappointment to go away.

The letter from Kate's grandmother Morrison had been written way back in October when they were still on the trail. Kate's mother read it out loud. Aunt Agatha was laid up with aching joints. The nights were bitterly cold already with a few flakes of snow.

The man who bought their farm had a pleasant wife who came over to chat in a neighborly way. She didn't mention missing them but sent her love and blessings.

Her mother opened the second letter with a cry of delight. "Kate," she said. "This is from Sarah Lauder who was so kind to us in Oregon City."

Kate could almost hear Mrs. Lauder's faintly Scottish speech behind the words her mother read aloud. Mrs. Lauder had so much enjoyed the pleasant visit with Jane. She wished her and her family the most joyful of holiday seasons. "And listen to this!" Jane said.

" 'Please plan on visiting with Mr. Lauder and me. I keep telling Mr. Lauder that we must drive out so he can meet you nice people. Don't be surprised if we show up on your doorstep some sunny afternoon. In the meantime, do write. I'd be charmed to hear from you.' "

Amy's letter was written on the lined paper Kate remembered from school. It was full of news about parties and her new clothes for school and how mean the new teacher was to all the girls because she liked the boys best. "I still use the embroidery scissors you gave me," Amy wrote, "and I think about you a lot. Please write back and tell me about Oregon."

"How nice of Amy," Kate's mother said. "You must do as she asks. The practice at writing will be good for you."

Just seeing Amy's handwriting and reading her words brought her friend back vividly. Kate remembered how bright Amy's eyes were and how quick she was to laugh at every funny thing that happened. There wasn't much time for letter writing, but Kate loved thinking of things to tell Amy in her own letter. She found herself making up sentences in her head that she wanted to put in.

But the letter would have to wait until after Christmas. Molly had been counting the days. When she got down to the fingers on one hand, Simon sharpened his axe and called Kate and Tildy to follow.

"Christmas tree time," he told them. "I'm not going to pick it out all by myself."

They found the perfect tree almost at once. It was taller than Kate and Tildy but shorter than Simon. It was perfectly shaped and looked almost decorated already with tiny brown cones clustered on its branches.

Bird appeared and watched Simon cut it down.

"Want to come help us trim it?" Tildy asked Bird.

"How?" Bird asked. "You mean with candles like at the Mission?"

"Candles cost too much and Papa is afraid of fire," Kate told her. "We just put pretty things on it."

While Simon nailed the tree to a stand, they started making ornaments. Kate cut some of her drawing paper into strips to make a paper chain. Molly couldn't use the scissors, but she spread flour and water paste on the strips and held them together until they dried into little loops. Tildy folded squares of the paper and cut out snowflakes that she fastened to the tree with bits of thread. When Kate's mother tied bright little bows on the branches, the tree looked beautiful.

"It's perfect!" Jane said, smiling at them.

Bird shook her head. "Need one more thing," she said. "I know what!" Her bright eyes sparkled. "Can Bird use your little baskets, Kate?"

When Kate brought her three tiny baskets, Bird unfastened her necklace. She removed nine tiny, speckled shells and put three in each basket. Then she set them carefully in the limbs of the trees. "See? The tree needs nests! Like outside."

Jane Alexander smiled at her and knelt at her side. "I have a gift for you, Bird." Bird stared, clearly not knowing what to say. "Close your eyes and hold out your hands."

Bird caught her breath as if with fear, but obeyed. The gift was small and round and wrapped in crinkly paper. She looked down at it, then up at Jane.

"Take the paper off," Jane said. "See what it is."

Bird's mouth fell open as she unwrapped a tiny round mirror. "This is my own?" she asked.

"Your very own," Jane said. "So you can see the

171

pretty Bird we all love so much." She hugged Bird, then smiled as Bird turned the mirror in her hand and peered at her face in it.

"I don't know how to thank," Bird said, holding the little mirror tightly between her palms. Her cheeks were flushed with happiness.

"You don't have to thank me," Jane told her softly.

Once the tree was up, the days rushed by. They all had last minute things to do. Tildy sewed buttons on her father's shirt while Kate finished the sampler she had started for her mother. Jane made a cake from dried apples with the butter Jackson had bartered from a neighbor. Sam snared a salmon to be baked in the coals, and Kate's father shot a great goose to roast.

Kate had never been able to sleep on Christmas Eve for as long as she could remember. That Christmas Eve was the worst. The house smelled of everything good she could think of — the pine scent of the tree, the spices, the sage of the dressing. Even Miss Porter seemed restless, grunting softly once in a while.

Just about dawn on Christmas morning, Buddy barked a few times. It didn't sound like his bark to warn of danger but more like the way he greeted a friend. Kate shot out of bed anyway, remembering the night her father had shot at the golden cat. Her father was at the door by the time Kate reached the window.

"Merry Christmas, Buddy," he said as the dog shoved against him with his morning greeting. "What do you say, old fellow? Did we have an early morning visitor? Come look at this, Jane."

Kate's mother, with a shawl over her nightdress, was just behind him. She cried out softly and clasped her hands together. "Oh," she said. "How beautiful. And they have to have come from Bird!"

The woven wooden basket was filled to overflowing with sprays of wild roses, their petals still damp with the night dew. Jane lifted the basket and carried it inside.

"Merry Christmas," she told Kate and her father softly. "A merry Oregon Christmas, with winter roses."

Kate had not seen Bull Thompson since the day of Titus's funeral. The sadness in his face made her chest hurt. Like the others, he gave the holiday greeting and shook hands all around, but his eyes were haunted by pain.

Molly didn't even complain that Miss Porter, complete with a red ribbon around her neck, had been banished to the fenced yard. She was so eager to open the presents under the tree that she bounced on her bench all through dinner.

Finally the meal was over and Molly, as the youngest, got to hand the presents around. Everyone got gifts they liked. Tildy shed her boots and put on the stockings Kate had made her at once. She had saved her father's gift until the very last. Kate held her breath along with Tildy as he unwrapped the big package. Tildy had insisted on making the shirt all by herself, not even letting Kate's mother help. It *had* to be right. It couldn't be another "honey pie."

Bull lifted the shirt and held it up. It was beautiful. The collar lay just right and buttons marched straight down the front between the generous pockets.

"Now *that's* what I call a shirt," Bull said proudly.

Then he held it against his broad chest. Tildy gasped. Everyone could see that the shirt couldn't possibly fit around her father's bulk.

"Well, I tell you, Tildy," her father said. "The only thing I'd rather have than a shirt for myself is one for my boy here. You try it on, Buck."

Buck took the shirt and measured it with his eyes. "I couldn't take anything this nice-looking away from Jackson. Here, you try it."

Kate's ribs hurt from how hard she was pressing her arms to her sides. It *had* to fit someone. It *had* to. It was so beautiful and Tildy had worked so hard on it! But it was clearly too small for Jackson's great shoulders.

"I would take it with pride," Jackson said. "But that way I'd be the only one to enjoy it. Paw, I think you should give it to the twins, so twice as many of us can enjoy it."

Tildy flew to her father's arms, fighting tears. "Oh, Paw," she cried. "I wanted so much to make something you'd like."

He patted her back with his broad hairy hand and held her close. "I couldn't like anything more than I like that shirt. And look at Simon there putting it on. I can't *see* a shirt I'm wearing. This way I can really enjoy it."

Tildy turned and looked at Simon. He struck a pose like a dandy in a picture, with one fist on his left hip and his other hand pretending to hold a cane.

Jane Alexander rose and took Simon's arm. "Now that is what I call handsome," she said.

Tildy giggled and buried her face in her father's chest.

"There's only one more present," Jane said. "It's for you, Kate, from your brother."

She drew a tiny wrapped package from her apron pocket and handed it to Kate. Kate's fingers trembled as she tugged at the paper. From Porter? How could that be?

"He gave it to me to save for this day," Jane said

softly. "It made the long trip to be here for you."

Before the paper was all the way off, Kate knew what it was. The tiny case held a pair of embroidery scissors like the ones she and Porter had picked out for Amy Lyons almost a year before. She clasped the case to her chest, giddy with happiness.

17
Glory Day

Kate held the tiny scissor case between her hands. Past time swept over her the way the great foaming waterfall above Oregon City leaped its dark ledges to swallow the sky.

Almost a year had passed since she gave Amy Lyons the exact twin of these scissors for her birthday present. She could still hear Amy's squeal of delight and her promise to "wear them forever to remember you by." Amy had taken the red cord that she wore around her neck and fastened the scissor case to it, before slipping it under her belt.

Amy had said in her letter that she still used the scissors and thought about Kate.

Amy had no idea how different Kate was now from the "best friend" she remembered. Would they even be good friends now? When Kate answered Amy's letter and told her the important and funny things about her life, would Amy understand them? Probably not.

In fact, Kate giggled to herself as she imagined

Amy reading such a letter to her mother and to Kate's other old friends. She could never put into words how outrageous and wonderful Tildy was. What would they think about Kate having an Indian girl named Bird for a friend? Would they even believe that Bird could run like the wind and make baskets you could hold in your hand? Would they think it was funny that little Molly had a pig who wore a bonnet and slept in the house? Could they even imagine the deep woods wreathed with rainbows lying in the shadow of towering snowy mountains?

It didn't matter really. That snowy day in Ohio was etched in Kate's own memory like the clusters of frost patterns that had decorated her Ohio bedroom windows. Her friendship with Amy belonged to her yesterdays but would always be warm in her memory.

What mattered was her brother Porter. *He* remembered her. She knew for a certainty, holding the tiny scissors, that he not only remembered her, but had sent his love ahead all those months and all those miles so she would remember, too. Her friendship with Amy might only belong to her yesterdays, but Porter was forever, and forever had all kinds of tomorrows in it.

Molly, always the lover of small things, leaned against Kate, touching the tiny case with a careful finger. "Oh, Molly," Kate whispered softly for fear

Tildy might hear and be offended. "We have the nicest brother in the whole wide world."

Molly's cheek was damp and a little sticky as she leaned it against Kate's face. "I have the nicest sister, too."

Kate stared at her and stiffened. "Oh," she cried. "Oh, my goodness, Molly. I plumb forgot." She eased Molly off her lap and shot to the back of the cabin where her mother kept the linen trunk. In all the excitement of the presents and good things to eat and winter roses from Bird, she had forgotten the present she had made for Molly herself all those weeks before.

It was too dark in the corner to see inside the trunk. "Tildy," she called. "Would you please bring the candle for just a minute?"

With Tildy kneeling beside her, Kate dug in the trunk for the bright red stocking she had knitted, then filled with presents for Molly. When she didn't find it at once, she began setting things out on the floor.

"I remember this," Tildy said, lifting a piece of cotton. "This is the dress you ruined the day we went after honey."

"Mother only saved the good scraps," Kate said without looking up. The stocking was clear at the bottom and she pulled it out carefully so as not to spill anything.

"This doesn't look like just a scrap," Tildy said,

holding up the piece of cloth and shaking it out. Kate stared at it. The calico had been cut up and sewn back together again. It looked like a little night-dress, too small for a person but too big for a doll like Annabelle. She lifted the candle and stared at the pile of things she had laid out. There were *two* of the little calico dresses, and a tiny knitted cap, and a soft shawl with fringe.

Both families were gathered before the hearth. The Thompson boys lay or sat tailor fashion on the floor. Sam was laughing at something Buck had said. Kate's mother and father shared the narrow bench. Bull Thompson sat alone, his face solemn, staring silently into the dancing flames.

Kate got up and took the little garment over to her mother. "Look what I found," she said. "Whatever is this tiny dress for?"

The room was suddenly so silent that a burning log slumping on the grate made a distinct sound. Buddy, sleeping in the cool draft by the door, raised his head and yawned noisily.

Kate's mother gave a little cry. She took the garment swiftly and folded it between her hands as if to hide it. Her face flushed scarlet, and she seemed to have trouble finding something to say.

"Whatever were you doing prying around in my trunk?" she asked, her tone sounding more embarrassed than reproachful.

"Looking for Molly's Christmas stocking," Kate said. "I forgot I had it for her."

"A stocking!" Molly cried, taking it from Kate's hand. "Oh, look!" she cried. She made a lap of her skirt for the things inside the stocking. Her voice became background sound, like rain against a window, as she took out the little treasures and talked to them, one by one. Her voice rose and fell in a constant happy singsong. She didn't even think of giving the fan to Annabelle. Instead, she fanned herself, brushing the downy owl feathers against her own round cheeks.

Nobody listened to Molly's happy prattle. Although the Thompson boys stared at the fire, Kate could feel their attentions riveted on her mother. Bull Thompson didn't pretend to look away. As he stared at Jane Alexander, a slow smile lit his eyes, then changed his face. "Lady Jane," he said softly.

Then he rose. His great body blocked off the light as he took both of Kate's mother's hands in his. "I do declare," he said gruffly, suddenly needing to cough a little. "Now *that's* what I call a Christmas present. A new life bringing joy back to where it was lost."

Kate couldn't breathe. Tildy caught her hand and squeezed it so hard that tears almost came. Kate's father nodded and smiled. "Well, there goes *that* secret," he said, grinning as broadly as a boy. "And the world no worse off for the telling."

Then it was true. When Kate's mother nodded and looked away embarrassed, Kate felt whole rainbows of joys explode inside her chest.

A baby. A baby of their very own.

She and Tildy rushed to hug Jane, almost tumbling her off the bench. She held them very close for a long moment before she let them go. Kate didn't want her mother ever to let them go. She certainly wasn't going to go anywhere with Porter or anybody else for any reason at all.

Their very own baby would come to this cabin and these deep woods. This baby would be an Oregon baby, different from herself, different even from Molly. Who else could tell this child how it was to grow up in Ohio? Molly was a child of the trail with few memories of any other home. But it all belonged to this baby even as they all belonged together. This would be home, home always. Most of all, the cabin with its solid walls and pine-scented air was the only place she ever wanted to be.

Tildy grabbed Kate's hand and tugged her toward the door. "Come on," she whispered. "I just got to dance!" Buddy shot out of the door with them, his tail wagging furiously at the joy of escaping the heated cabin.

The woods were darkening with evening and the birds were loud in the trees. The smoke from the new chimney rose, then curled around the top of the clearing as if it would rather not leave so happy a place. They startled an owl from the tree above the woodpile to sweep off into the darkness. Miss Porter and her brothers grunted their complaints at being awakened. Kate and Tildy didn't care. With the great dog cavorting around them, they whirled and circled and laughed until they both had tears running down their cheeks, and the first star of evening rose at the top of a towering pine.

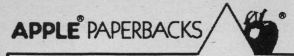

APPLE® PAPERBACKS

Pick an Apple and Polish Off Some Great Reading!

BEST-SELLING APPLE TITLES

- ❑ MT43944-8 **Afternoon of the Elves** Janet Taylor Lisle $2.75
- ❑ MT43109-9 **Boys Are Yucko** Anna Grossnickle Hines $2.75
- ❑ MT43473-X **The Broccoli Tapes** Jan Slepian $2.95
- ❑ MT42709-1 **Christina's Ghost** Betty Ren Wright $2.75
- ❑ MT43461-6 **The Dollhouse Murders** Betty Ren Wright $2.75
- ❑ MT43444-6 **Ghosts Beneath Our Feet** Betty Ren Wright $2.75
- ❑ MT44351-8 **Help! I'm a Prisoner in the Library** Eth Clifford $2.75
- ❑ MT44567-7 **Leah's Song** Eth Clifford $2.75
- ❑ MT43618-X **Me and Katie (The Pest)** Ann M. Martin $2.75
- ❑ MT41529-8 **My Sister, The Creep** Candice F. Ransom $2.75
- ❑ MT42883-7 **Sixth Grade Can Really Kill You** Barthe DeClements $2.75
- ❑ MT40409-1 **Sixth Grade Secrets** Louis Sachar $2.75
- ❑ MT42882-9 **Sixth Grade Sleepover** Eve Bunting $2.75
- ❑ MT41732-0 **Too Many Murphys** Colleen O'Shaughnessy McKenna $2.75

Available wherever you buy books, or use this order form.

Scholastic Inc., P.O. Box 7502, 2931 East McCarty Street, Jefferson City, MO 65102

Please send me the books I have checked above. I am enclosing $_____ (please add $2.00 to cover shipping and handling). Send check or money order — no cash or C.O.D.s please.

Name _____

Address _____

City _____ **State/Zip** _____

Please allow four to six weeks for delivery. Offer good in the U.S.A. only. Sorry, mail orders are not available to residents of Canada. Prices subject to change.

APP591